Where Dolphins Race with Rainbows

~ *Tales of Karensa* ~

Jean Cullop

Scripture Union

By the same author
Tales of Karensa: Castle of Shadows
Tales of Karensa: Children of the Second Morning
Tales of Karensa: Silver Serpent, Golden Sword

Scripture Union, 207–209 Queensway, Bletchley,
Milton Keynes, MK2 2EB, England.
Email: info@scriptureunion.org.uk
Website: www.scriptureunion.org.uk

Scripture Union Australia
Locked Bag 2, Central Coast Business Centre, NSW 2252
Website: www.scriptureunion.org.au

Scripture Union USA
PO Box 987, Valley Forge, PA 19482
Website: www.scriptureunion.org

Printed and bound in Great Britain by Creative Print and Design (Wales) Ebbw
Vale.

Cover design: fourninezero design

Scripture Union is an international Christian charity working with
churches in more than 130 countries, providing resources to bring the good
news about Jesus Christ to children, young people and families and to
encourage them to develop spiritually through the Bible and prayer.
As well as our network of volunteers, staff and associates who run holidays,
church-based events and school Christian groups, we produce a wide range
of publications and support those who use our resources through training
programmes.

Contents

4

The song

There is a land for broken dreams,
A place the aching heart knows,
Where sea birds fly from rocks of gold
And dolphins race with rainbows.

Where woodland creatures freely roam
The healing stream of peace flows.
Release your heart to find that place
Where dolphins race with rainbows.

Fisher village

Harbour

Farmland

Luke and Rosie
arrived here

Tobias
farm

High
Hill

Dark Forest

Narrow track

Black Rock
Bay

road

road

Carrik's
house

Farmland

Coastal path

Fields

road

King's
Palace

Dark Forest

Bellum's
Castle

Ford

Stream

Kett's house

River

Meadow
of
Flowers

Moors

Bay of
Dolphins

Farms

The far side of the island

Town

Farms

Bay of
Perils

Karensa

Chapter 1

Rough seas

The dinghy moved smoothly down the creek towards the open sea. Luke gave a steady pull on the oars so that the blades splashed into the water in perfect time.

He was old enough to know that it was dangerous to take the boat too far from shore, but today Luke didn't care. He wanted to get as far away from Dad and Stacey as he could, even if that meant taking a huge risk.

He told himself that the little holiday craft was light and easy to control. He'd had plenty of practice on the park lake at home so he knew how to handle a rowing boat and the sea was unusually calm today, still, beneath the cloudless blue sky. The slight breeze was just enough to ripple the surface of the water so that the sea shimmered in the bright sunlight. The same breeze ruffled his fair hair and Rosie needed one hand free to keep her long curls from getting in her eyes.

Luke was certain he had everything under control.

Rosie, who was three years younger than Luke, was not so sure. She could just about manage two lengths of the swimming pool but the boat was now way past the furthest headland. She knew that she would need to be careful what she said to her brother if she was not to send him off into an outburst of temper...

"The beach is a long way off now," she murmured lamely.

Luke ignored her and pulled even harder on the oars. The last thing he wanted now was Rosie nagging him.

"Luke..."

Steely grey eyes glared at her.

"I know what I'm doing, Rosie. I can handle a boat, you know, and besides, I didn't ask you to come!"

Rosie's lip trembled in spite of her efforts not to cry. Sometimes she was just a little scared of her older brother. Even though he had stuck up for her when she was being bullied at school, she had a feeling it was because he liked to get into a fight, not because he cared what happened to her.

Most of the time he and his friends were rude and noisy and the neighbours were always complaining about them.

Once he had been in trouble with the police. Rosie never found out why, but soon after the police had been to their house, Dad and Stacey had got married.

Rosie had been bridesmaid. She had worn a long pink dress that secretly she thought was really sad and made her feel stupid, but she kept quiet rather than spoil Stacey's day.

Stacey had looked like a princess, everyone had said so. Everyone, that was, except Luke, who spent the whole day scowling.

Dad and Stacey had come to Cornwall for their

honeymoon, leaving Luke and Rosie to spend a boring two weeks being looked after by Gran who treated them as if they were still babies and took them for walks in the park. Luke hated it.

Then, when they returned home, Dad and Stacey made the shock announcement that they were all going down to Cornwall to live. They had sold their big semi-detached house in the Midlands and bought an old fisherman's cottage at the head of a long, narrow inlet called Poldawn. Dad soon found a job in a nearby boatyard and they were meant to be one big happy family starting a new life.

Only so far it hadn't worked. And with Luke in his present mood it was not going to work either.

Rosie glanced over to him. His face told her that he knew full well that she was scared, but it wasn't going to make a scrap of difference. She would just have to sit tight and hope that he decided soon to turn back although right now she guessed that turning back was the last thing on his mind.

Luke wanted to be home with his friends. He hated Poldawn, he hated Cornwall and he hated Stacey most of all.

The trouble was that Luke still remembered their Mum and Rosie didn't, well, not really because she had been so young when Mum had died.

Luke could put a voice to the tall, fair-haired young woman in the photograph that used to stand on the dining room unit at home. Dad no longer had the photo on show now that he had married Stacey and they'd moved house. The photo was still in one of the packing cases without a permanent home.

Rosie's memories of Mum were mostly from things she had heard other people say.

Luke felt a pang of guilt. Rosie looked scared. He shouldn't really have come out so far.

"We'll go back soon," he promised.

Rosie relaxed and gave him a watery smile. "The people on the beach look like toy figures, they're so far away. This is like being in our own special world," she said, then she added, "Luke, let's go back."

"In a minute," he promised. "My arms ache. Your arms would ache too, if you were rowing. I just need a rest. The tide's going in so we won't go any further out to sea."

"It might change. The tide turns about this time of day."

Luke sighed, impatient again. "It won't change yet. Ten minutes Rosie, that's all."

He knew that he'd be in big trouble when they did get home. Dad had forbidden him to take the boat any further than the end of the creek.

There was still this morning's argument to sort out, and all over a bowl of cornflakes. Stacey had tried to save money and bought a cheap kind. Luke wanted a brand name and he'd given voice to his opinions of the cornflakes and of Stacey – very loudly! Stacey ended up crying. Luke grinned at the memory of it. It was wicked!

Dad had been really angry then. "She's only trying to help. She's doing her best to fit in with the family."

"I don't want her to fit in!" Luke had stormed. "She isn't Mum! She won't ever be Mum!"

He'd run out of the cottage and clambered into the little dinghy that was moored at the end of the garden.

When Rosie followed him he was surprised, but he didn't have time to argue. He just knew that he had to get away. If Rosie wanted to tag along, that was up to her.

Rosie had surprised herself. Maybe, deep down, she felt sorry for him. He was her brother after all, and Stacey wasn't any relation, even though Rosie did quite like her.

Tired out, Luke rested on the oars. He closed his eyes against the sun and leant back on the boat.

Suddenly he was back in the house where they had lived when he had been small. He was in the garden and he must have been very young because Mum was pushing him on the swing while Rosie played in the sand pit. The swing went higher and higher and he was scared. He looked over his shoulder to Mum but he couldn't see her face.

Then she called to him in the soft, low voice he remembered so well.

"Find the place, Luke – the place where dolphins race with rainbows..."

He wanted to ask her what she meant but the words got muddled in his throat.

"Luke... Luke... Luke... wake up!"

As he forced himself to open his eyes, the dream vanished and it was Rosie calling his name, not Mum. He wanted to go back to sleep, to dream the dream again, but there was an urgency in his sister's voice that told him he had to wake up.

He shivered. The sun had disappeared. In its place a grey mist had rolled in, completely hiding the shore. With the mist had come a wind and the little boat was rocking from side to side.

Now it was Luke's turn to be afraid.

"We'd better get back!" he gasped.

"Back where? Where is back?" Rosie wailed. "Luke, we can't see a thing! We could row and go further out to sea. We don't know which way the boat is facing!"

Luke swallowed hard. She was right. To move the boat now could easily take them into even more danger.

As he looked around, desperately trying to decide what to do, the sea made the decision for him and they began to move, as if being pulled along by a sudden underwater current.

Luke made a grab for the oars, but it was too late. They slipped out of his hands and disappeared into the water.

Rosie was crying. "Luke, we're going to drown!"

"Shut up Rosie, of course we won't!"

They clung to the side of the boat as it rocked crazily through the water, riding the surf at an alarming speed. Then suddenly it was over.

Neither of them saw the huge wave before it hit the boat with a great crash.

Luke tried to grab his sister as they were tossed into the water, but the sudden cold drove every breath from their bodies.

It was useless to try to swim against the current. Luke felt the sea pummelling him. There was no sign of Rosie. Salt water was in his mouth. He was unable to hold his breath any longer.

His last memory was of a huge grey shape moving towards him.

And then it was dark.

Chapter 2

Karensa

"Welcome to Karensa."

Luke opened his eyes, blinking against the strong sunlight. He was sprawled on his back on soft, dry sand. In front of him the sea was calm and deepest blue, the waves lapping gently against the shore.

So the mist and the storm were a dream? He was safely back at Poldawn.

But as he struggled to sit up he realised that there had been no dream. This was not Poldawn. This was a bay of clean, flat sand surrounded by cliffs, lush with flowering plants and bushes unlike anything he had ever imagined.

What was more, he was being watched by a group of the strangest looking people he had ever seen.

They all had long hair. The men wore theirs loose to their shoulders but the women and girls' hair was braided into several plaits and decorated with coloured ribbon. Men and women were dressed alike in long belted tunics, loose trousers and soft boots.

Stories of desert islands and cannibals flicked across Luke's mind.

"Welcome to Karensa," the voice repeated as one of the men came and knelt by Luke's side on the sand. He reached out his hand and touched Luke's wet T-shirt and shorts and clipped hair and the boy suddenly realised that he looked as strange to these people as they did to him.

Luke stared curiously, at the same time drawing back from the man's touch. He seemed to be quite old. His hair and beard, although dark, were streaked with grey. His eyes were sharp and brightest blue like the sea.

Suddenly the memory of the storm and the grey shape in the water came back to him. He struggled to sit up.

"Rosie...?"

"Your sister is quite safe." The man pointed to an outcrop of flat rock to their left and sure enough Rosie was there. When she saw that Luke was recovered she waved to him. She seemed to be wrapped in a huge cloak and was drinking something from a rough beaker.

So they had both survived!

"We didn't drown then," he murmured, more to himself than anyone else. "Why didn't we drown?" The man pointed again, this time to the open sea. "Telki and Praze saved you," he told him.

Luke scanned the waves but all he could see were two dolphins at play.

Dolphins... why did the thought of dolphins stir his memory?

The man went down to the water's edge and held out his hands. Then he gave a strange call, high pitched but soft. At once the two dolphins swam close and stood high in the sea, chattering with a clicking sound.

"Telki and Praze are saying they enjoyed saving you," he told them, laughing.

Luke stared in disbelief. "You mean you understand what they're saying?"

He nodded with a grin. "More, or less! Come, we should go to your sister."

He pulled Luke to his feet, but Luke was not prepared for the way his legs turned to jelly. He shook all over and the beach was tipping crazily from side to side.

The man put a steadying arm around his waist.

"When Telki brought you in you were very close to drowning," he said kindly. "You need to rest. Karensa will give you the rest you need."

Luke hesitated. He had no intention of trusting these people and no intention of staying here any longer than he needed. Part of him still thought that this was all a dream and part of him thought that the sea had landed them a few miles down the coast from Poldawn. These people must belong to some weird community and the quicker he and Rosie returned home the better.

It seemed the man could read his thoughts. "Karensa is an island," he explained, "And I am called Josh. I am the leader of the fishing people of the island. You are both welcome to share my home. You may eat and sleep until you are recovered... Not many find their way to Karensa and the island will be your home for as long as you have a need."

Luke frowned. What need? The only need they had was to get out of here.

As he puzzled over this, Rosie came and stood by his side. She looked so funny, wrapped in a huge cloak with just her small, very wet head sticking out, that Luke laughed in spite of himself.

"You see, Karensa is already bringing laughter,"

Josh smiled and this brought the customary scowl to Luke's face.

With Rosie was a tiny, dark-haired girl carrying another beaker of liquid.

"This is Delfi," Rosie told him.

Luke took the beaker. Delfi nodded but did not smile.

"Delfi is my daughter," Josh explained. "She is shy and not used to strangers. When she knows you she will talk... But take her drink, it will restore you."

Luke stared at the beaker. The liquid was thick and yellow like custard, which he hated. Yet it tasted of lemons and strawberries and apricots. And it did revive him. His teeth stopped chattering and he stopped shaking.

Delfi took back the cup and Josh, after dismissing the small crowd of spectators, indicated that Luke and Rosie should follow him up the cliff path.

They exchanged glances. What should they do?

Luke shrugged to her unspoken question. "What choice do we have?" he whispered in her ear. "Don't worry, Rosie, just as soon as we can get away, we're going home."

Josh smiled to himself.

Rosie pushed aside one of the huge flowering plants that grew across the narrow cliff path. The way was steep and she struggled for breath. Josh and Delfi, on the other hand, seemed to have no problem and were striding well ahead, for the first time out of earshot.

"Where are we, Luke?" Rosie gasped.

"How should I know?" he snapped. "At least we

didn't drown." He laughed harshly. "He says two dolphins saved us."

"They did, Luke, they did save us! I rode on Praze's back. High up above the waves!"

"Do you remember what happened then?"

"Of course I do... Telki brought you in but the sea got to you first... I thought you were drowned!"

"Well I'm not! And as soon as I can, I'm going home, and I don't mean to stupid Poldawn either!"

Rosie sighed. Why couldn't her brother be like he used to be, before Stacey came on the scene? He was OK then. Or, why couldn't Luke get on with Stacey like she did?

They had reached the top of the path. Josh and Delfi had stopped and were waiting for them.

"That's funny," Rosie said, "The sun's still shining and it's warm and the sky is still blue, but Luke, we can't see the end of the water."

She was right. A mist obscured the horizon.

"Karensa is always surrounded by mist," Josh explained, then added mysteriously, "That is why only the chosen ones find it. And those who do may only leave when the day comes."

"You mean we can't just go?" Rosie asked.

Gently, the man put one hand on each of their shoulders and looked down at them. His face was very kind.

"Karensa will be your home for as long as you need it. When your need is met, a way will be made for you to return to your family. Until then you must stay here."

They thought about his words. Delfi slipped a small hand into Rosie's hand and she smiled.

"It's all right, Delfi," Rosie said softly. "I'm not afraid. No, I'm not, Luke. I want to go home to Dad but I'm not afraid."

Luke bit his lip, deep in thought. It was true. It seemed that there was nothing on Karensa for them to fear.

"There is no fear on Karensa," Josh told them. "You will soon realise that this is a very special place. Our King rules us with perfect justice. All who are in trouble may go to his Palace each day at dusk and there the King makes judgement."

"What if he judges wrong?" Luke wanted to know.

"The King is never wrong. His word is our law. Even the King himself is not above his word. He always stays true to his laws and keeps every promise that is made in his name... But see, we are home."

They were facing a low, stone cottage facing the sea. Behind the cottage was a moor and behind that a forest.

Delfi took their hands and urged them to go forward towards the cottage where a woman stood waiting for them.

"My wife will have food prepared," said Josh and Luke was suddenly reminded that he was very hungry indeed.

Just as they reached the cottage door they heard a dreadful sound, a sound greater than the west wind and deeper than thunder and it came from the dark forest beyond the moors.

At once Josh, Delfi and the woman dropped to their knees and bowed low to the ground.

Rosie copied them, but Luke remained standing,

in spite of Delfi tugging at his hand and whispering that he should do the same.

"It must be the King! Bow down, Luke!" Rosie cried.

"It's not the King," said Josh, "It's the Lords Veritan and Bellum, the Lords of the King's Palace. Show some respect for them, boy, and get to your knees!"

Chapter 3

The three thrones

The sound, greater than the west wind and deeper than thunder, ceased as the riders drew their horses to a halt.

Luke's knees hurt. He was kneeling on a stone. He was wondering how long they would be expected to stay like this when a voice spoke to them, a voice of strength and power.

"You should not kneel to us, we are only servants of the King. To him alone you must bend the knee. Get up, all of you."

Luke pulled himself to his feet and helped Rosie who seemed unable to move.

They were magnificent. One had hair dark as midnight and wore a scarlet cloak over a black tunic. The other had hair as pale as silver and was dressed in blue. Both had circlets of gold over their long hair and neither had a beard. They carried swords, and their feet were clad in high boots of finest leather. Precious jewels sparkled from their belts, their wrist bands and the clasps on their cloaks.

Their horses were no less splendid. The dark Lord's horse was black and pawed the ground, neighing softly. The other was grey and waited patiently.

The dark haired Lord spoke. "Oh, I don't know,

Veritan," he said in a slow, lazy drawl. His voice was soft and musical. "I think we should be worth a bent knee or two, don't you?"

"We are servants," his companion repeated. "None should bow the knee on Karensa except to the King."

The other one shrugged and laughed, but there was no laughter in his dark eyes. They were hard and cold.

The fair one spoke again. "I am Lord Veritan. This is Lord Bellum. We are both Lords of the King's Palace and enjoy the King's confidence. The King has heard of your arrival and has sent us to fetch you. He will see you during the Time Of Decisions."

"You mean your King wants to see us?" Rosie gasped.

Luke nudged her. "You should call him sir," he hissed.

Lord Veritan didn't seem to mind. "Of course he wishes to see you. Our King is concerned for all the people of Karensa."

"But we're not..." Luke began, but thought better of it. After all, you didn't argue with Lords, did you? Certainly not when they were as powerful as these.

Lord Bellum, the dark one, inclined his head. "You will come with us now. It will be evening soon and the Time of Decisions will be ended."

Josh cleared his throat. "Lord Bellum, the children are still wet from the sea and they have not yet eaten."

"They must come now," Bellum insisted. "The King will not be kept waiting."

Veritan agreed with him. "They will be given food and their clothes will dry naturally. The girl will come with me. The boy with Lord Bellum."

Luke and Rosie allowed themselves to be hoisted up on to the big horses in front of the two Lords. Veritan's arm went around Rosie, holding and protecting her, but Bellum sat well back so that Luke could grasp the horse's mane.

"We haven't said thank you," Rosie whispered to Veritan.

"Child?"

"To Josh and Delfi. We didn't thank them for helping us."

"They will not expect thanks," Veritan replied.

"At home we have to say thank you," Luke added. "It's good manners."

"You are not at home," Bellum said harshly. "These people would consider it an honour and a joy to serve you. They would be insulted by your thanks.... Now hold on to the horse's neck. The hour grows late. We must go."

Faster and faster they sped, further and further into the Dark Forest, the horse' hooves making a sound greater than the west wind and deeper than thunder. Trees rushed past them.

Luke clung to Bellum's horse. This ride was the best ever, more thrilling than any theme park white-knuckle ride. His whole body had come alive with excitement.

Rosie, riding behind them on Veritan's horse, was laughing out loud, and this from someone who had been sick on the pirate boat at the theme park.

But they were not scared.

Luke peeped over his shoulder to Lord Bellum, but his dark eyes were expressionless. Neither he nor Veritan seemed to be affected by the speed of the ride. They were most likely used to it. They probably did this every day, Luke thought.

Then, quite suddenly, they stopped.

They had cleared the forest and were looking across open fields. Beyond the fields, only a mile or so away, high on an outcrop of granite rock stood the Royal Palace.

"A fairy castle!" Rosie gasped.

"Hardly," Bellum said. "Child, there are no fairies here on Karensa." And he laughed in a mocking way.

"Of course there are not," Luke said scornfully, maybe because Bellum's laugh made him feel uncomfortable. "There's no such thing as fairies, Rosie. Surely you don't still believe in fairies, do you?"

Rosie's lip trembled. "It does look like a fairy castle though."

"Yes it does," Veritan agreed kindly. "Well, it looks like the castles in the books of your world. See, it has turrets of gold and pennants of silver. But you must not compare them, child. And boy, you should not mock your sister."

Luke felt his face go red and he would have liked to make an angry reply, but the spirit of his heart told him that Lord Veritan could be just as fierce as Bellum appeared to be.

More slowly now, they moved across the field, then uphill, until they clattered through the gates into the courtyard.

The castle was like nothing they had seen or could ever have imagined. The walls and floors were made of marble yet at the same time they shone with a pale silver light. The light was everywhere, reflecting from the pillars and vaults of the great hall. Each pillar was decorated with a coloured banner and the bright colours fused into the silver light.

Now that they had dismounted, they realised that Veritan and Bellum were huge, probably twice their height or more, so that Luke and Rosie, who walked in behind them, seemed very small and unimportant.

At one end of the great hall were three thrones of black marble and on the centre throne sat the King. The silver light shone from his face and about his person and he was dressed in gold from head to toe. The golden crown, over his long, grey hair, flashed with rubies, emeralds, sapphires and diamonds and many other jewels that the children could not name, like amethyst and topaz. The jewels shone and sparkled, casting dancing patterns of rainbow light on the marble floor. His face was ageless, although he had a grey beard. His eyes shone with wisdom and knowledge.

Veritan took Luke and Rosie to one side where many people, quite ordinary people it seemed, were waiting to see the King. Some were dressed finely in silken tunics but others, like the man they stood next to, seemed poor.

"You must wait until your name is called," Veritan told them and then he and Bellum took their places on the other two thrones.

The King spoke in resonant tones and the power

of all creation was in his voice.

"Let the swords be drawn!" he commanded.

At once Veritan took his sword from its scabbard and held it high. The golden blade flashed and sparkled.

"The Sword of Truth," he declared.

Bellum followed him, but his sword was of black steel.

"The Sword of Justice!" was his cry.

Luke watched, breathlessly. Everything now was forgotten except for this. Nothing seemed as important as this King and this strange island. He dismissed any lingering thoughts that they may have discovered a strange community. This was much, much more.

Something puzzled him, though. There seemed to be someone else here, someone he couldn't quite see, standing behind the King's throne. He couldn't understand this, he only knew in his heart that someone else was here.

The King held up his hand. "Let truth and justice reign! May wise decisions be made!"

Slowly, the line of people began to move towards the three thrones. As they did so, an expectant hush fell upon the gathering.

Chapter 4

Tobias

Luke and Rosie stood in line, as one by one, people went to the King for problems to be resolved and hopes restored. Soon it would be their turn and they had no idea what to do or say.

Rosie's knees were knocking. Luke only kept from trembling by focusing his eyes on the man in front, who had a slightly bent back and seemed very poor because his tunic was patched and darned. He also smelled of farmyards. Luke wondered if he had come for money or new clothes. Or maybe a bath?

This last thought made Luke laugh out loud and the man turned round.

"Be silent, boy, or you shall be taken from the court," he growled. He spoke with a heavy accent, not unlike that of the Cornish people of Poldawn, and his face was weather-beaten and plain. The front of his tunic was patched more than the back.

Luke decided to ignore him. It seemed that not everyone on Karensa was as kind as Josh and Delfi.

At that moment his stomach decided it was hungry and complained loudly.

The man turned round again and this time he said nothing. Instead he pinched Luke's arm.

Luke gasped and rubbed his red arm. Anger welled inside him at the undeserved punishment.

He was about to throw caution to the wind and tell this man just what he thought of him. He didn't care if he was in the presence of a king.

It was just as well that, at that very moment, the farmer was called forward.

He shuffled forward. Luke did not feel sorry for him at all. His arm hurt where the man had pinched him. But he was curious to know why the man had come, so he listened hard.

The farmer knelt before the three thrones.

"Lord King, my name is Tobias. I am a poor farmer from the other side of the forest, near the fisher people. My farm is not large, but the ground is good and yields a fine crop."

"Then what is your problem?" Lord Bellum asked, obviously trying to hurry the man. Luke stifled a laugh and heard Rosie giggle behind him so he glanced over his shoulder to let her know that he agreed.

"Lord King, as I said, I am a poor farmer from the other side of the island," Tobias went on, refusing to be hurried. "But at present, things do not go well for us. I was late with my harvest and the Time of Gathering is over. My crops are ruined and we have no grain for the Time of Snows."

"Why were you so late?" Lord Veritan wanted to know.

"Lord King, we went to visit our family on the far side of the island and we stayed longer than we should. By the time we returned home it was too late. The Time of Gathering was ended."

Veritan spoke to the King. "We cannot let his family starve, Lord King, even though he was foolish."

Tobias hung his head and shifted on his knees. The floor must have been very hard.

Rosie would have felt sorry for him, if she had not seen the way he had hurt Luke for no reason. He couldn't help his stomach rumbling. She was hungry too.

"He should have made plans!" Bellum was saying. He did not seem as kind as Veritan. Rosie hoped that when it was their turn, Veritan would help them.

The King held up his hand for silence. "This is my judgement... I am a King who desires to meet all his people's needs. Give this man grain from the Palace store. Give him just enough for his needs and no more. Tobias, in the future you must make provision for your family. This must not happen again."

"No, Lord King, it shall not," said Tobias, bowing his head in shame as a servant ran off to obey the King and find grain for him to take home.

As Tobias moved off, the King called out, "Are there no more for justice?"

"Only the strangers, Lord King," Veritan replied.

"Then I must see them now. Let them come forward."

Rosie grabbed Luke's arm and held on very tightly as they walked up to the three thrones.

"Tell the King your names," Bellum ordered.

Luke opened and closed his mouth but no sound came out. It was Rosie who spoke for them both.

"My name is Rosie, Sir, and this is Luke, my brother."

Luke regained his voice. "Lord King, you should have called him Lord King," he hissed in her ear.

"Then come forward, Rosie and Luke. We do not

often see strangers on Karensa."

They heard a ripple of interest from the people watching and suddenly felt very odd in their T-shirts and shorts, even though they were now dry. Rosie's fair hair had dried with the salt water still in it and was tangled and matted into tight curls.

There were five steps to the King's throne and Luke's knees wobbled on every one. He had never been in awe of anyone before, certainly not teachers, nor his dad.

They knelt by the throne as they had seen the others do, but then, as Luke lifted his eyes to the King's face, all his fears melted away, There was nothing to fear from this King. It was his goodness that made him so awesome. He made you want to kneel to him. It seemed the right place to be.

"Luke, you tell me where you are from."

Luke swallowed. "From Poldawn, Lord King, that's in Cornwall, well it's in England, actually. Only we don't really belong to Poldawn, that's just our new home. We have another home, and that's in England too." He felt he was making a mess of this. "There was a storm," he added. "A wave hit our boat and we capsized and ended up here..."

"And do you know why you are here yet, Luke from Cornwall in England?"

"No, Lord King," Luke said, shaking his head.

"I see," the King said gravely. "Well, the fact is you are here, so what are we going to do with you?"

"Please," Rosie whispered, "Please, Lord King, we would really like to go back home. Our Dad will be getting worried. He'll have the police out by now."

"You cannot go home yet, Rosie," the King replied. His voice was very gentle but it did not allow them to argue. "You cannot go home until you find out what really brought you here. Then a way back will be found. And do not be concerned for your family. They will not be searching for you."

There was a pause.

"Are you King Arthur?" Rosie asked suddenly and for no real reason. She couldn't think what put the thought into her head. At once she wished she hadn't said it.

A big smile spread over the King's face, although Bellum and even Veritan seemed dismayed.

"No, child, I am not King Arthur. But I am a great King, greater even than him. I have more than Karensa at my command."

"I just thought..." Rosie's voice tailed off. She would have liked him to have been King Arthur. They had been reading about him at school. He had lots of knights and a round table and the knights went around saving maidens. That could have been fun...

"Where is the farmer, Tobias?" the King wanted to know.

"Here, Lord King." Tobias came forward carrying two sacks of grain.

"Farmer Tobias, I have a task for you. This is my judgement. You have received of the King's mercy this day. Now you have a chance to pay back what we have given to you, although of course you do not have to. My gifts are free. However, you may feel that you want to help."

"Anything, Lord King."

"These two strangers... Will you take them into your own household, Tobias – oh do not be concerned, we shall increase your portion of grain – will you care for them as your own?"

Luke's heart fell into his shoes. He wanted to cry out that they would sooner go to Josh and the fisher people but he was not to be given a choice.

"Yes, Lord King, I will," Tobias replied, no longer ashamed. "I have two children of my own. The strangers will learn our ways from my own family."

"Then take the children into your home. Treat them exactly as you would your own. If your children work, then these must work. If they play, then these should play. If they are rewarded, then these must be rewarded and if they are punished, then these must be punished."

Luke saw Rosie's lip tremble. She was going to cry. He had already tasted Tobias's punishment and it still hurt. And that was before he had done anything wrong.

At that moment, Dad and Stacey and Poldawn seemed the best place in the world. And they might never return.

It was no use protesting. Here, the King's word was law.

As they turned to go, Luke was again sure that there was someone else standing behind the King's throne, yet when he looked no-one was there.

They loaded the grain, now increased to three sacks, into a small cart harnessed to a very old brown donkey.

Tobias indicated that they should get into the cart

with the grain, although there was room on the driving seat.

So far, Tobias had not spoken, but as they moved off, he turned and looked at Luke over his shoulder.

"You shall do well with me, boy, if you only do as you are told. My wife shall be kind. My children are of goodly character. But you shall be treated as they are and must learn respect. I will feed you and care for you but you must work as all farm children work. And you must obey me and my wife and also my children until you learn our ways. Do you understand me?"

Luke went to reply, but, at that very moment, his stomach growled again.

Anger flashed in Tobias's eyes. He stopped the cart and turned round.

"What is that rude noise you make?" he cried. He raised his hand, as if to strike Luke, but Rosie sprang to his defence.

"It's because we're hungry! We can't help it! We haven't had any food all day!"

"What, nothing at all?"

"Not even a bowl of cornflakes," Luke said gloomily.

"Boy, I don't know this cornflakes, but I do know that it cannot be good to eat nothing at all. When we get home my wife shall give you good bread and cheese... And I do beg your pardon for hurting you before... I had no thought of what such a strange noise should be. I never have been quite without food...We must get you home and fed... And into some proper clothes!"

Luke and Rosie exchanged glances. No way were

they going to dress like these people... No way!

But, even as the cart rumbled into the Dark Forest, they knew that they would have to do as they were told.

Chapter 5

The house by the Dark Forest

This journey through the Dark Forest was so different to the exciting ride with Veritan and Bellum.

The donkey was old and slow and the cart rumbled clumsily over the woodland track, bumping Luke and Rosie from one side to the other. The only light was from the full moon that hung very low over the island.

Tobias remained silent. Either he was concentrating on where he was going, or he did not want to talk to them, or maybe he simply had nothing to say.

Luke and Rosie crouched down behind the sacks of grain and whispered in the darkness.

Luke spoke with a confidence he did not feel. "Don't worry, Rosie, we'll get home. Soon as the mist clears."

"When will that be?" she whispered.

"We'll have to keep watch. Sea mist never stays that long, does it? As soon as it clears we'll find our boat and go back to Poldawn."

"We don't have any oars."

"We can soon make some! We can cut down trees or something. We can't stay here. This place is weird!"

Rosie paused. "But I liked Josh... and Lord Veritan... and that King... I don't know about Lord

34

Bellum..."

"I enjoyed the ride on his horse. We went like the wind... But they're all weird... OK... but weird... It's like we went back in time."

Rosie gasped. "Maybe we have?"

"No," Luke shook his head. "They all seem to know about how we live at home. No, it must be some crazy history project or something."

"Do you think Dad will ever find us here? I've never heard of anywhere called Karensa, but it might be on his map of Cornwall. And he's sure to be searching."

Luke did not reply. He could not see how anyone would ever know where they were. And he had been looking at Dad's road map only the other day. He was sure that there was no such island as Karensa.

The sudden breath of sea air awoke them with a start. They had left the Dark Forest and were taking a narrow track along the cliff where the fisher people lived.

They passed by Josh's house. Rosie wished they could have stayed there. She liked Josh, and Delfi too, even though she found it difficult to talk to strangers. They could have become friends.

Tobias was not at all friendly. Rosie didn't like him one bit.

Once past the fisher houses the road turned back towards the forest again and came to a big, grey, rambling farmhouse. A light shone in the downstairs window and they could hear the sound of voices from inside.

Wearily they climbed down from the cart and

Tobias led the way inside, still without a word to either of them.

The sudden warmth made Luke feel dizzy and he grabbed hold of the door to stop himself from falling over.

Rosie helped him to sit down, taking charge, although he was older and bigger than she was and twice as strong.

"We're hungry!" she cried defiantly. "And my brother nearly drowned! He needs care!"

From a long way off, Luke heard a soft voice reply.

"Then care he must have. And food for both of you... whoever you are."

Kind hands lifted a beaker to his lips. Once again it was that thick, yellow liquid that tasted of fruit and looked like custard and once again the mixture revived him.

Feeling better he looked around.

The house seemed poor and old-fashioned. It reminded him of the open-air museum Dad and Stacey had taken them to last summer where a whole street of houses had been reconstructed to show how people had lived in times gone by. There was no television but the wooden table was laden with food and some kind of stew was simmering over an open fire.

Three pairs of eyes looked curiously at them. The woman must be Tobias' wife and the others his children, a girl of about his own age and a boy a little older. All three had red-gold hair that shone in the light from the lantern. Their skin was pale and their eyes the lightest green.

"My family," Tobias said, finding his gruff voice

at last. "My wife Martha, my son Petroc, my daughter Morwen."

Martha surveyed them, hands on hips. "Why husband, you went to the King for grain and see what you have brought."

"I brought plenty of grain," Tobias replied and he grinned in a startling sort of way. "These are two strangers to Karensa."

"Strangers? My dear life we do not often see strangers." Martha chuckled. She was a small, plump, round sort of woman. In her brown tunic and trousers she reminded Rosie of a plump brown hen.

Tobias nodded. "The boy is called Luke. The girl is Rosie. The King himself asked that we should take care of them in exchange for extra grain. Well, it was not exactly like that, but no matter. They both need food and a wash... oh, and proper clothes to wear."

Martha beamed. "Why that is honour indeed, that the King should trust them to us. He must think well of you, husband... Welcome Luke, welcome Rosie. I think the food should come first, then the wash. I shall find you clothes that Petroc and Morwen have outgrown. Come now, we shall all take supper together."

Luke found himself sitting next to the boy, Petroc who seemed fascinated by Luke's short hair.

"Why is your hair cut off?" he asked.

"It's how everybody has their hair cut." Luke replied indignantly. He looked at the other boy's shoulder length red hair. "Nobody has long hair now; it went out years ago," he added, stressing the point.

"We do."

"Well, it might be OK here, but it's not the fashion in England."

"In your world?"

"Yes, we must get back there really soon. Our dad will be worried about us. Once that mist clears we'll have to go."

No-one replied. The boy Petroc looked at the floor. Tobias sat down at the table.

Rosie thought that maybe they should be more polite. After all, these people were looking after them.

"Morwen, that's a nice name," she said. She was surprised to see the girl blush. She must be shy. Rosie and Luke both stared at her, a little rudely. Neither of them had ever known a person who was shy.

"Thank you," Morwen murmured softly. "I was named for my grandmother."

Martha gave them each a generous portion of what seemed to be vegetable broth and told them to help themselves to the warm crusty bread and white cheese.

Luke looked for a spoon. There was none. He waited to see what the others did and then copied them and drank it straight from the bowl.

He grinned in spite of himself. "Stacey would throw a wobbly at this!" he exclaimed.

This was fun. The soup dribbled down his chin and he mopped it up with a crust of bread. The food was good, but it made them tired. Rosie was trying not to yawn.

Martha said firmly, "Now for a wash."

Much too tired to argue they followed her into a

tiny scullery where a tin bucket of water was being kept warm over another fire. She poured water into a bowl.

"While you clean up I shall find you clothes."

When she had gone Rosie whispered, "I don't want to wear those things, Luke."

"Neither do I, but we don't have any choice."

Rosie brushed her eyes with the back of her hand. "Luke, I want to go home. I want to see Dad, and Stacey. I don't want to stay here."

He was just about to make an angry reply when something stopped him. After all, she was only nine years old. This was the first time she'd complained. Not once had she blamed him for what had happened even though it was his fault they had gone out so far in the boat. And she had defended him when they had arrived at the farm and he felt ill.

Awkwardly he put an arm about her shoulders. "Rosie, we'll go as soon as we can. And these people are kind. They'll take care of us, I'm sure."

"Not Tobias,"

"Well, not so much him. But the others are nice enough."

Martha came back then with a brown outfit for Luke and a blue one for Rosie. When they put them on they found that they were surprisingly comfortable, light and warm and not itchy like their salt encrusted T-shirts and shorts.

"Now your hair," Martha said to Rosie.

Rosie gasped. "You're not cutting it?"

"No, my dear, why should we do that? But it needs braiding, so it looks nice and keeps tidy. Morwen shall do it for you."

Rosie sighed. There was no point in arguing, and

besides, she was too tired, so she sat patiently while Morwen gently combed and plaited her long, fair curls into three braids, twisting blue ribbons into each braid.

"There, that does look well on you," Morwen said at last. She was right. The plaits suited Rosie's small, round face.

Rosie yawned again.

Martha saw it and said that Petroc and Morwen should show them their beds.

"And I shall need to speak with my dear husband to see how we shall all live."

A loud snore told them that her dear husband was already asleep in his chair.

The boys' bedroom was low and square with a window under the eaves. Petroc could only just stand upright.

For tonight they would have to share a straw mattress and rough woollen blankets but it was warm and dry.

Petroc spoke to Luke before they went to sleep.

"About your leaving... Well it will soon be my thirteenth year and I have to say as I never once saw that mist rise."

Chapter 6

Brothers at sunset

From High Hill, Luke could see most of the island, the Dark Forest behind the farmhouse, the fisher houses and the boats moored in the bay below, and other farms and cottages scattered over hills and fields. On the other side of the forest, in the distance, he could see the turrets of the King's palace. Most of the coastline was visible from here, including the bay where the dolphins had brought them to land.

Sometimes they had seen Telki and Praze leaping through the waves but they never stayed long, preferring the deep water of the far ocean.

This was Luke's favourite place on the island. He never tired of watching the sunset on Karensa. It did not sink below the sea but instead faded softly into the mist, first red, then orange, then palest pink until it disappeared. He would imagine that Dad could see the same sunset back at Poldawn.

In the two months since they had come here, Luke had changed. His skin was tanned from working in the open air and his arms and legs more muscular. His fair hair had grown and, if he stayed much longer, it would soon reach his shoulders. In his brown tunic and trousers and soft, high boots he looked no different to the Island boys.

Luke had changed inside too. He had been forced

to learn patience as each day there was still no hope of leaving Karensa. He was more friendly towards Rosie again, now that Stacey was not around. And he had learnt not to lose his temper at the least little thing. Like Rosie, he was beginning to accept that here he had a new life until they could go home.

Tobias and his family worked hard. Even Rosie was expected to work, although most of the time she stayed at the farmhouse and helped Martha.

Tobias was not as they had first thought. True, he never had much to say, but he was fair and never seemed to tire of showing Luke how the work must be done.

Once, when they were hedge-cutting, Luke really messed things up and made a gap in the hedge big enough for the sheep to get through. Tobias did not shout at him, but simply showed him how to collect the cuttings and mend the hole.

"You do well, boy," he said in his gruff way. "But you need to take time. Your world is all busy and rush. It won't do here."

"Do you know my world?" Luke asked curiously.

"Oh, enough I do know. Televisions, computers, that I know."

"Why don't you have them here?"

Tobias shrugged. "Have you lacked anything since you came here, boy?"

"No... no, I've missed some things, like television... and my play station... and burgers and chips."

"Well, soon will be the Time of Snows when we may rest from work. Petroc shall take you into the Dark Forest, where the snow lies deep, and teach you to sledge down the hills. Then you will come home and we shall tell stories as we sit by a great log fire."

"What do you do at Christmas?"

"Christmas? Why, we don't have Christmas on Karensa."

One time the four of them, Luke and Rosie, Petroc and Morwen, had all gone blackberrying. Their baskets were overflowing with soft, black fruit and their mouths stained red with the juice. The sun was warm and they were tired and they had sat on the grass at the bottom of this very hill.

A rabbit came close by.

"He's so tame!" Rosie exclaimed. "He's not afraid of us at all!"

"Why should he be afraid?" Morwen asked.

"We don't have fear on Karensa," explained Petroc.

The little animal continued to look at Luke, his head first to one side and then the other.

Luke sighed heavily. "Why are you always so unhappy?" asked Morwen in her quiet voice.

"It's because we can't go home," Luke replied.

"At home you were unhappy too," Rosie sighed.

"Not with home, not with Dad. Just with... with..."

"Stacey," his sister prompted.

There was a long silence then the rabbit hopped off, jumping right over Petroc, who just laughed.

Not all the times had been good.

They were all forbidden to climb down to a cove called Black Rock Bay. Tobias told them it was dangerous. The black rocks were slippery and the tides unpredictable and they were all, including Petroc, told they were not to go there.

Luke wanted to go down to the cove. Maybe it was because he had been told not to. The beach was scattered with shiny black rocks. They were just asking to be climbed over.

"Come on, Petroc, no one will know. We could have a great game."

The older boy hesitated. "Father does say there is great danger there. The tide comes in so quick, one minute you're on the beach, the next you're in the sea."

"That's the fun of it. If you're not too scared!"

"I'm scared of nothing," Petroc declared. "We'll go down."

They had a great time, jumping from one slippery rock to the next and climbed back up the cliffs only to find Tobias waiting for them at the top.

He looked so angry. He took them both by the arm and marched them straight back to the farmhouse.

"You will go one to the hay loft and the other to the barn and stay there until I shall send for you."

They did not argue.

For a day and two nights they stayed where they had been put with no one to talk to. Luke found that when he had time to think about it, he was sorry that he had led Petroc into trouble. Petroc had been a true friend.

Now, sitting on High Hill, Luke thought about these things. He was glad when Petroc threw himself on the grass beside him.

"Luke, I knew I should find you here."

"Every day I watch for the mist to clear, yet it's still the same."

Petroc looked sad. "So you still hate us? Mother and Father are kind to you... and... I thought we were friends."

"We are."

"Brothers almost? I never had a brother before... Or even a true friend. I know lots of people, Luke, but none are real friends."

Shocked, Luke realised that Petroc was lonely, just like himself. He had mates at home, but more often than not they got him into trouble. Or he got them into trouble.

"We could be brothers... if you want..."

"Blood brothers?" Petroc asked eagerly.

"Well... maybe not that..."

"Very well. Give me your hand... From now on, Luke, you shall be my brother."

"And you mine, Petroc."

Once, Luke would have been embarrassed by words like those, but here, tonight, it seemed the right thing to do.

For a long time they sat there, looking out over the sea.

"The mist won't go," Petroc said at last. "Not until the time is right, Luke."

"When will that be?"

"You'll know.... Come. We should go back to the farm. The sun is fading fast. Supper will be ready."

"My dad watches the sunset," Luke said slowly, without making any attempt to get up. "I think it makes him remember Mum..."

He had never talked like this to anyone.

"Do you miss your mother?"

Luke felt unexpectedly angry. "Why did she die? Why did she leave me?" he cried. "And Dad... Dad... Oh no!"

"What? What is it?"

"It's Dad. I can't remember what he looks like! I'm not stopping here any longer. I've got to get home! I'm going to that King now and telling him he can't keep us here any longer."

"You can't do that!"

"Oh yes I can. I'm going now, before it gets dark."

Petroc bit his lip. It was a habit of his when he was making a decision.

"Very well," he said at last. "You should not do this, Luke. The King's judgement is always wise. But if you are set to go, then I shall go with you, brother."

Chapter 7

The forest of fear

The Dark Forest was comforting as night fell on them. The tall trees protected them and night creatures, owls, badgers and foxes followed their route in a way that felt encouraging and kind, while thousands of glow-worms lit their path. Friendly eyes watched from the ferny undergrowth as woodland creatures made sure they were safe.

Petroc was suddenly curious about Christmas. They never had Christmas. What did they do in Luke's world?

Luke was glad to talk of other things. Now that they were on their way to see the King he did not feel so brave.

"Well... we eat a lot, plenty of chocolate and nuts and fruit... we play games sometimes, like scrabble and stuff... we watch loads of TV... oh, and we have a Christmas tree with lights and put presents underneath."

"A tree? In the house?"

"Only a small one. We plant it in a pot and decorate it with tinsel and things."

"Then what?"

"Well... nothing really. That's about it. Why don't you have Christmas here?"

"We do have the Feast of Snows."

"What's that?"

"We all gather at the King's Palace for a party. There is music, and games, and dancing too, if you care for it. We have hot chestnuts and baked potatoes and sweets and hot spicy drinks. It goes on all night until dawn. Of course," he looked sideways at Luke, "If you do go home then you shall both miss it."

"So?"

"I shall miss you both if you go; so will Morwen."

Luke began to struggle for words. "It's not... I mean... I just... we don't belong!"

"You could belong," Petroc said quietly. "Father, he says you have come here for a cause."

"What cause?" Luke cried scornfully.

"That I do not know, brother... But you say you must go?"

Luke thought of that brief few moments when he had forgotten what Dad looked like.

"I must go," he said firmly.

"Then I shall help you. See, we are nearly there."

Back at the farm, Rosie was worried. It was dark and still Luke and Petroc had not returned home. They had missed supper and Luke never missed supper.

She knew where he had gone. To the High Hill to see if the mist had cleared. He thought only of going home.

Rosie wanted to go home too, but she was not unhappy here. Like her brother, she now looked like any other islander in her blue tunic and trousers, her high boots and braided hair. She confided her fears to Morwen as they stood together by the open window.

Morwen did not seem unduly alarmed. "Petroc is sensible, they will be safe." she whispered softly.

"He wasn't sensible when they went down to Black Rock Bay. You don't know Luke. If he wants to do something, nobody can stop him."

She was surprised when Morwen blushed. She was no longer shy with them. Maybe she liked Luke more than they knew?

Morwen bit her lip, just like Petroc did when he was worried, and Rosie guessed that really, Morwen was also concerned.

There was a strange atmosphere tonight. A sort of unease. Karensa knew nothing of fear, yet tonight it was as though something was about to happen, something not good.

Even the animals sensed it. The dogs were waiting watchfully by the door and the cat was pacing restlessly around the kitchen instead of sleeping in her usual position in front of the fire.

The girls stood by the open window and would stay there until their brothers came home.

Their brothers, though, were a long way from home; they were at the King's Palace and tonight at the Time of Decisions there seemed to be more people than usual to see the King.

Just as before, Veritan and Bellum sat on either side of the King, their swords raised high for truth and justice. The King seemed even more splendid than he did the first time Luke had seen him.

Two women were being judged and they appeared to be arguing. They each held part of a fine cloak of deepest crimson wool, decorated with coloured braid and beads.

The King, it seemed, was not pleased. He signalled to the two Lords of the Palace. Quickly, and none too gently, Bellum stepped forward and separated the two women.

"You do not behave so in the presence of the King," Bellum roared thunderously. "We, of the King's household, must be honoured and obeyed."

Veritan seemed to be trying not to laugh. "Tell the King your problem... You first," he pointed to the younger woman.

"My Lord," she said in a voice that trembled, "I am Zena, married to Tas the woodcutter. I spent so long making this cloak to warm me in the Time of Snows, but this woman, my husband's sister, Nolis, is claiming it as her own!"

"It is mine, Lord," the other woman pleaded. "I made the cloak." She turned towards Lord Bellum. "Surely, my Lord, you can see I am honest?" And she bowed low before the dark-haired Lord of the Palace.

Bellum seemed to grow in stature as she bowed to him.

"I believe she is honest, Lord King," he said.

A ripple of laughter passed through the watching crowd, but the King did not smile.

"Bellum, give the cloak to me. And give me your sword."

Bellum obeyed.

"My judgement is this. The cloak shall be cut in half. They shall have half each. Do you accept this judgement?"

Nolis folded her arms in a defiant gesture. "I do, Lord King."

"No... No..." Zena cried. "Lord King, let Nolis

have the cloak. Do not destroy it!"

Now the King smiled. "Zena, you have proved the cloak is really yours. Rather than see all your hard work destroyed you would give it to your sister-in-law. Here, the cloak is rightfully yours."

Bellum was not pleased. "Lord King, that is not fair judgement!" he objected. "How can we be sure this woman is not lying?"

A great gasp, almost a sigh, passed around the great hall. Briefly the light seemed to fade, then come back. In that instant, Luke was sure he saw another person standing behind the King's throne, but then he disappeared. Maybe he had just imagined it.

No one had ever dared to question the King.

The King was on his feet. When he stood up, although he was no taller than Veritan or Bellum, he seemed to tower over them.

"That is my decision, Lord Bellum! Give Zena what is rightfully hers and let them go. I will see the next person. The hours pass and I will see all who have come to me before the Time Of Decisions ends."

He sat down again and this time a middle-aged man, finely clothed in a tunic of deep purple, trimmed with fur, walked up to the steps of the three thrones.

He bowed elaborately.

"Sir, I am Carrik. I own many of the farms and cottages on Karensa. I am not able to pay the King my dues as one of my tenants has not paid me. What shall I do?"

"Why has this man not paid you?" Veritan asked.

"He says his harvest failed, Lord."

"That is no excuse," said Bellum. "This man should be made to pay you what he owes so that you can pay your dues. Send strong men out to collect the rent."

The King held up his hand for silence. "Not so! Landlord, I am willing to cancel your dues to me on one condition. You must forget what this man owes to you."

Bellum's face darkened with anger, but he did not dare argue again.

"Yes, yes Lord King," Carrik said eagerly." That is only right and fair."

He went away smiling and clutching a scroll which was the King's pardon.

It was the boys' turn. Now that they were actually here, things did not seem so easy. No matter how wise and just the King was, he was still the King.

He seemed surprised to see Luke again.

"Is Tobias not treating you well?" he wanted to know.

"Yes... yes, Lord King. This is his son, Petroc... We have become friends."

"Then why have you come to me?"

Luke began to feel foolish. Petroc was not a great deal of help either. This was the first time he had been to the King's Palace and his eyes were everywhere, except where they should be which was on the King.

Luke cleared his throat nervously. "Lord King... I want to... I want to go home," he said in a voice that was no more than a whisper.

He had nothing to fear. Only the disobedient need have fear of this King.

The King beckoned to them. "Come, both of you, come up here. Come close."

At last Petroc seemed to realise what was expected of him and together they climbed the marble steps and stood, trembling, before the great high throne. The light from the King's face seemed to calm and comfort them.

"Boy," he said to Luke, "you know that you cannot leave Karensa until a way is made through the mist. Now that could be tomorrow, or it might not be for a very long time. It may be that you have work to do on Karensa. Or it may be that Karensa has something to teach you. Until then you must be content to stay where you are."

Luke was disappointed. But then he looked up into the King's face and his heart began to race for he saw such love and compassion as he had never known. Truth and justice were there, with youth and age.

Suddenly he realised that what had happened to him and Rosie was exactly right; that it had been planned before all time. He knew that Karensa was no ordinary place and that this was no ordinary king.

This was a King he would be happy to serve all his days.

After the Time of Decisions was over, Luke and Petroc stood outside in the courtyard with some of the others who had been to see the King.

"Petroc... your King.."

"Our King, Luke."

"OK, our King then... who is he?"

"He's the King, of course," Petroc replied, laughing.

"But where does he come from?"

Petroc shrugged. "He has always been King. And always will be, I suppose."

A sudden disturbance behind them made them turn round and listen. It was the two women with the cloak and they were still arguing.

"I don't consider the judgement to be fair!" Nolis grumbled loudly. "The cloak was mine!"

From the shadows came another voice as Lord Bellum joined them. His dark eyes gleamed with anger.

"I would have cut the cloak in half," he said softly. "Shall I do so now?"

Zena gasped. "That would be disobeying the King!"

"So?" Bellum sneered, still in that same soft voice. "Is the King always right? Does he always tell the truth to you? I tell you this, there are mysteries he keeps from you... You, landlord, are you going to forget this man's debt to you? I could give you men to collect it."

Carrik hesitated, then said, "Why should I forgive this man? No, he shall pay me what he owes."

Petroc, who usually had little to say, and would sooner listen than talk, now joined in.

"We cannot disobey the King!" he declared.

Casually, Bellum pushed him to one side with a single movement of his arm.

"Be silent Petroc, son of Tobias! Do not ever make an enemy of me. As for you others, I am grown tired of the King's ways. I will rule this island as is my destiny. You will worship me and I will reveal to you truths hidden since before time."

Luke joined in. "You should not go against the

King. He's a good King!"

"What would a stranger know?" Carrik snarled.

Nolis found time to drag her envious eyes from Zena's cloak. "Yes, keep your opinions to yourself!"

Before Luke could think of a suitable reply, a mighty wind swept over the courtyard, so that they could hardly stand against it.

Lord Veritan stood at the Palace gate and with him the King.

The King's anger was terrible. He gave a roar like a great lion in pain, wounded in battle.

"Bellum, you are no longer a Lord of the Palace! Go from this place and never return!"

Bellum did not cringe. Boldly he faced the King.

"If I go, then others shall follow me!"

"So be it. Go!"

Furiously, Lord Bellum called for his horse, and when a trembling servant brought it from the stable he leapt on its back.

With a single call to his followers, and flourishing his sword, he rode from the palace.

A third of the King's household left with him.

Luke and Petroc walked home in silence. The forest no longer seemed friendly. Eyes watching them now made them uneasy.

All about them they could hear the sounds of Bellum and his friends, as they crashed through the undergrowth, and the cries of animals fleeing deeper into the forest for safety.

Fear had come to Karensa.

Chapter 8

Carrik

Rosie snuggled down beneath her blanket. She did not want to get up today.

When Luke and Petroc had returned home late the previous night, they had told of Bellum's rebellion. Tobias had said that Karensa would never be the same again. Now it was she, not Luke, who was anxious to go home.

Luke had changed last night. He seemed stronger, almost grown up, and he and Petroc had been talking about how they were going to fight Bellum. Thoughts of home had disappeared. Rosie didn't understand.

Morwen, lying next to her, was wide awake.

"What are you thinking about?" Rosie whispered.

"Only such as happened yesterday. All night the deep forest was filled with such sounds..."

"What do you think they were doing?"

Morwen shuddered. "I do not care to think. Rosie, I never heard such sounds before... The animals were wailing and fleeing for their lives. I have never known them to behave like this before."

"What has happened, Morwen?"

"I do not know... I do not feel we can ever go to the King again."

Rosie puzzled over this and then she realised that for the first time ever, the people of Karensa were experiencing fear.

A sudden noise brought them wide awake and shivering to the window. Men were hammering at the door. They were all Bellum's followers.

Quickly the girls threw on their clothes and ran downstairs but Tobias, Petroc and Luke were there before them.

"It's the landlord, Carrik, the one the King saw yesterday," said Luke.

Tobias was talking to him.

"I cannot pay the debt, sir," he said. "I have had to rely on the King myself this year for grain."

"The King?" Carrik laughed. "What King is that? There is no King as far as we are concerned. We serve Lord Bellum. Come man, pay the money you owe."

Petroc gasped indignantly. "The King forgave your dues only last night and said that you should do the same. That was his judgement."

Carrik and the three men with him all laughed. Carrik had a harsh, nasal laugh that seemed to scorn everything and everybody.

"That King's judgement means nothing now. He is finished. We are Lord Bellum's men and many more shall turn to him. Their numbers increase by the hour. That King is no more."

"We shall never join Bellum!" Tobias cried. "The King is still ruler of Karensa. We, at least, will remain loyal!"

Martha had joined them and stood beside her husband. "My man speaks for me too," she said stoutly, "Me and my household."

"So be it," Carrik said slowly. "Pay me the money you owe me."

"I do not have it," Tobias admitted.

"And you have no right to ask for it!" Petroc protested.

"I have the right given me by Lord Bellum. If you do not have the money then we shall take the payment in those two sacks of grain."

"Without the grain, we shall starve before the Time of New Birth is here," Martha said. "You cannot take our food from us."

"You two men, take one... no take two sacks of grain. One for their stubbornness."

As the men moved towards the grain store, Petroc tried to stop them. Immediately Carrik's sword was at the boy's throat.

Petroc's face was white but he showed no fear and for what seemed like for ever the man and the boy stared at each other.

Then Carrik seemed to come to a decision.

"You have a brave spirit, Petroc, son of Tobias. Too much spirit to die at the end of my sword. You will become servant to my household. There you shall learn our ways."

"I'll never learn your ways!"

"Oh you will, Petroc," Carrik said softly. "I promise you will."

Without further ado, Carrik's men seized the boy and he was thrown unceremoniously across Carrik's horse.

They watched them go. Morwen was crying softly. Luke was too angry to cry. Besides, he had not cried for years. Now was not a good time to start. He could hardly believe these things were happening. He dared not think of how Carrik might treat

Petroc, but he guessed it would not be with kindness.

Rosie was crying too. "I want Petroc to come
home!"

"Shut up, Rosie!" Luke shouted, and that made
her cry even more.

Martha spread her plump arms around both of
the girls.

"What is done, is done. But one thing I do know.
We have one sack of grain to last for the Time of
Snows and it will not be anywhere near enough for
all of us," her voice trembled, "Even without
Petroc it will not be enough. I can only think that
Luke and Morwen will have to hire themselves out
for work."

Chapter 9

Where sea birds fly from rocks of gold

The farm seemed deserted with Petroc gone. The worst time was at supper. This had always been a happy, noisy part of the day, a time to share news about the day's work, but now it had become silent and sad.

Tonight was the saddest of all because tomorrow was the day the Hire Fair was to be held, so tomorrow Luke and Morwen would have to leave home to look for work.

Rosie's feelings were all mixed up. She felt guilty that she was the only one left at home, but she felt relieved that she did not have to go, yet she was still scared because Luke was leaving her on her own with Tobias and Martha.

She asked Martha if she could not go to the Hire Fair instead of Morwen who was, after all, their own daughter.

"No, child," Martha replied, giving her a sad smile. "The King decreed that you and your brother should be treated as our own family." She sighed deeply. "The least we can do is to obey him. So many in the Kingdom have deserted him to follow Bellum."

"A third of all those in the Palace have gone," Tobias told her, "Or so I did hear from the fisher people. It is only a few days since the rebellion, yet so many have joined Bellum. He rules them from his own stronghold between the Dark Forest and the Palace so that none shall reach the King. His men plunder and kill and steal. They have a new tunic decorated with Bellum's heraldic symbol, a coiled serpent. The Kingdom is lost."

"What about Lord Veritan?" Luke asked.

"Oh, he remains loyal. It is said he is eager to fight Bellum to the death but the King will have none of it."

"Why not?" Luke cried. "Look at the trouble Bellum has caused. If I were the King I'd have him put to death."

Tobias sighed. "Bellum was once the King's favourite Lord of the Palace. He still cares for him, even now."

Luke and Rosie did not understand this way of thinking. Neither, it seemed, did Morwen.

"Come, Rosie," she said. "We must clear the plates away."

Luke lay on his straw mattress, wide awake as morning broke. He was cold, for the Time Of Snows was nearly upon them, and he was lonely. When he had not been able to sleep he had always had Petroc to talk to. Now Petroc was no longer there.

He was scared for him too. Carrik would not be kind to any who remained loyal to the King.

The only sleep he'd had that night was troubled by dreams from which he would wake, shivering and too scared to either get up or go back to sleep. In the centre of the fisher village stood a cobbled square and it was there that the Hire Fair was held.

Luke and Morwen stood watching at first. After a tearful goodbye to Tobias and Martha – especially from Rosie – and a long walk along the cliff top, they were confused by the sudden crowds. They had hardly realised so many lived on the island of Karensa. It had always seemed a still, quiet place.

"Morwen," Luke said. "This place is different. It feels... it feels like back home..."

"What do you mean? Do they have Hire Fairs where you come from?"

"No... no it's not the Hire Fair... I don't know what it is..."

Bellum's men were everywhere. As Tobias had said last night, they had taken to wearing black tabards emblazoned with the coiled serpent. They even carried weapons, knives, clubs and swords.

The square was full and Luke found himself looking for Josh or Delfi but there was no sign of the people who had helped them, it seemed like a lifetime ago.

"Where do we go, Morwen?"

Morwen looked as scared as he felt. She had always been shy and quiet and only talked to those people she knew well. It must be hard for her to put herself up for hire with strangers, but she was trying to be brave.

"That must be the hiring stall over there, that wooden platform where those people are standing. Look, there are some children, Luke. We shall not be the only ones. Maybe Carrik has taken food from them all?"

"We'd better get on with it then."

"No wait... Luke... over there... it's Petroc!"

A cart had pulled up behind them and the driver was one of the men who had come to the farm with Carrik and taken Petroc away. They were taking provisions from a cottage while a woman and child stood helplessly by.

Petroc was being made to load the provisions while the man, armed with a wooden club, stood over him.

Luke caught his breath because Petroc seemed so changed. His red hair was uncombed and his eyes, which Luke remembered as being bright green, were clouded and dull. His face was white with dark circles under his eyes and he wore the hated serpent of Lord Bellum's household. There was a purple bruise on his cheek.

The woman at the cottage was crying and Petroc stopped what he was doing and spoke to the driver. Almost casually the man brought his club down across the boy's shoulders, so hard that he fell to the ground.

Morwen gave a cry and would have run to him had Luke not pulled her back.

"You can't help him that way! Bellum's men are everywhere! They'll take us too, then we'll never be able to help him!"

She became still. "But see how they are dealing with him, Luke. That's my brother! He never did anyone any harm in his life! Why are they treating him so?"

Awkwardly Luke put his arm about her shoulders. She was trembling.

"We'll rescue him, Morwen, I promise we will."

For what seemed like a long time they looked at each other. It was a promise he had no way of keeping. By nightfall they could both be serving in different houses. They might even have to work for one of Bellum's men themselves, though they had both sworn they would sooner starve first.

"If only the King were here," Luke sighed. "He'd know just what to do."

For a second he almost imagined the King was there with them, then the feeling left him. It resembled the feeling at the Palace, when he had thought someone was standing behind the King's throne. He shrugged off the feeling. It was something he could not understand. Petroc had struggled to his feet and stood swaying slightly, his head bowed.

"Don't let him see us," Morwen pleaded. "He'd be so ashamed."

"What of? It's not his fault."

"I know but... he would not want us to see him so..."

That day, standing in the line on the platform while men and women looked them up and down and discussed them as if they had no understanding and could not hear for themselves, had to be the worst day for Luke since they came here.

One by one people were chosen for hire and he and Morwen were the only ones left.

"Why doesn't anybody want us?" Luke whispered. "We're both fit and strong."

"That has nothing to do with it," she whispered back. "Some will not choose us because my father is loyal to the King. Others because Petroc works for Bellum's man, Carrik."

"What shall we do? We can't go back home and say we have no work."

As he spoke a man approached them, a man such as they had never seen.

His hair and beard were bright yellow, and both were long and unkempt, and his eyes were an odd turquoise blue, shining from his tanned face. He was tall, almost as tall as the Lords of the Palace and his clothes were of rough, brown wool. He wore a cloak of animal fur about his broad shoulders.

Morwen gasped. "It must be Kett!"

"Who?"

"Kett. He lives on the far side of the island and is so fierce none dares fight him, not even Bellum's men. And he did stay loyal to the King."

Kett was looking at them. His face was expressionless.

"You need work and a home," he said, and it was more an observation than a question.

Morwen nodded. She seemed unable to speak.

"I need help. I have food and shelter, poor as it be. I can keep you fed during the Time of Snows. Did you stay loyal to the King?"

Luke and Morwen nodded and then exchanged glances.

"Both of us?" Luke asked. "You'll take us both together?"

"I will that. The maid can cook and sew and you shall help me in my work, boy."

"What is your work?"

Kett did not reply and they had no choice but to follow him.

Kett lived a long way from the fisher houses. They did not dare to venture through the Dark

Forest; they had to take the coastal path around it, and they had a long, hard walk.

As they reached the far side of the island, the first flakes of snow started to fall. They began to shiver.

"You will need warm cloaks," said Kett, noticing their chattering teeth. "I will find some when we reach my home. See, we are almost there."

They rounded a sharp bend in the track and found themselves looking down upon a wide, rocky beach. Even though it was snowing the sun was setting in the way it always did on Karensa, fading slowly away, bathing the rocks in a golden light. Gulls and cormorants were everywhere, screaming mournfully as they dipped and dived for their supper.

"Look," Morwen breathed. "Oh look, the sea birds fly from rocks of gold."

Luke's heart began to thump very loudly, so loudly that he thought she must hear, but she appeared not to.

He remembered those words from somewhere.

"Where sea birds fly from rocks of gold..."

They reminded him of home...

Chapter 10

Salvis

Rosie stood with Tobias and Martha and watched as Luke and Morwen walked off together. They had no money, no food, not even a change of clothes.

No one knew when they would ever see them again.

"We had no choice," Martha said sadly.

Tobias placed a comforting arm around her shoulders. "They shall do well enough. I feel it," he replied. Neither Rosie nor Martha believed him.

There was work to do, but none of them had the heart to do it. Finally Tobias took the axe and went to split logs and Rosie, sensing that Martha wanted to be on her own, went to help him by stacking them up on the wood pile.

She shivered in spite of the hard work.

"The Time of Snows is coming," Tobias told her." In the past this has always been the best time on Karensa, but now..." He left the rest unsaid.

"What has happened?" Rosie asked. "What has gone wrong on the island?"

Tobias paused in his work and rested on the handle of the big axe.

"It is because someone has disobeyed the King," he said at last. "The King's rule was perfect, but now Bellum has brought us fear and death."

"Why doesn't the King fight back? He must be

stronger than Lord Bellum?"

"He is, child. Much, much stronger. But fighting is not his way. He wants his people to love him and serve him of their own free will... But there is talk of another, a deliverer who will restore the King... There is a man on the far side of the island, a man called Kett. I have never met him. He is a strange, wild man who lives alone in the caves among the sea birds... Kett is telling us to get ready for the coming of this deliverer, sent by the King... But it is only talk, I fear..."

"Will things be the same as they were before, when this man comes?"

"Child, they cannot ever be the same for what is done is done. But at least the King's law will be restored."

"And Luke and Morwen could come home... and Petroc..."

"Petroc too... Oh yes, Rosie, Petroc too."

The riders were upon them before they realised they were there; a group of Bellum's men led by the Lord himself and at his side was Carrik, the land-lord.

Rosie was scared. She was even more scared than she had been when their boat had overturned and the dolphins had brought them to Karensa. Only now she had learnt to control her fear.

Lord Bellum was a truly fearsome figure. He seemed so much bigger than he had done in the King's Palace. The emblem of the serpent blazed scarlet on his black tunic, worn now over a suit of chain mail. His sword was drawn and glittered with rubies and emeralds.

He sat proudly on his black horse and his eyes glowered down at them, changing colour from black to amber as the morning light flickered between sun and cloud.

Carrik, at his side, was almost as splendid. He too wore chain mail and a tunic of black and scarlet and like Bellum, his sword was drawn. He too was on horseback, a lighter horse than the one Bellum rode.

"You are Tobias, the farmer?" Lord Bellum thundered.

Tobias showed no fear although he must have felt it. "I am Tobias, sir."

"Well Tobias, I have come to tell you that I am disappointed in your lack of support for the New Order."

"I support the King, sir. To me the King is still and always will be the true ruler of Karensa."

Bellum's eyes became dark with fury. "I am the ruler of Karensa now. It is I, Bellum, you must support."

"That I cannot do, sir. Not while the King still lives in the Palace."

"That is your decision?"

"It is," Tobias said bravely. "And that of my household."

"Then you and your household must pay for your misplaced loyalty," Bellum cried. He turned to Carrik. "Let the men destroy this household!" he commanded.

"No!" Tobias sprang forward, swinging the big axe towards Bellum, but before he could use it Carrik brought the flat of his sword down hard upon the farmer's head.

Tobias fell to the ground without a sound.

Rosie heard her own voice screaming and the noise brought Martha running out of the farmhouse. She went to Tobias, but Bellum's men seized her and held them both so that they were forced to watch as the men set fire to the farm. Everything, including the cat and dogs, was destroyed.

Then they turned and, laughing cruelly, rode away.

Martha and Rosie ran over to Tobias who was lying very still.

"Oh Rosie," Martha sighed, "Tobias is dead."

The first flakes of snow began to fall as they knelt by the grave. Tears streamed down Rosie's cold cheeks but Martha's eyes were dry.

Rosie had not realised how much she had cared for this slow, quiet man with shoulders stooped from a lifetime of farming. He could be harsh, particularly when he had shut Luke and Petroc away for so long that time they had gone down to Black Rock Bay, but he was always fair, and he had taken in Luke and Rosie and given them a home.

On an impulse she took two sticks and, taking a red ribbon from her hair, she made the two sticks into a cross and placed it in the newly dug earth of Tobias' grave.

Martha looked puzzled. "What is that for, child?"

"I don't... well, I'm not sure... we have them at home... in church... Do you want me to take it away, Martha?"

"No... no, leave it. The red ribbon reminds me of the blood Tobias shed in serving the King." She lifted her head defiantly. "We should be proud of him. I will not be seen weeping for him, not me. I will not let Bellum have that victory. Wherever Tobias is now, Bellum cannot touch him. He's walking tall, Rosie. His back will be straight and he'll be at peace. Oh, yes, Rosie, he's walking tall. So we should not waste time weeping. Dry your eyes and together we'll finish the work he started."

Rosie did try to obey her, but a sudden, shocking thought started her crying again.

"Oh Martha, Petroc and Morwen need to be told. What shall we do?"

"I do not know." Martha sank back to her knees. "I do not know where we should go and what we should do and Rosie, I am suddenly very tired..."

She lowered her head. Her long red hair was well sprinkled with grey and all at once she did seem old.

Rosie took her hands to comfort her, but like Martha, she had no idea what they were going to do. The house was a burnt shell. They had no shelter, no money and no food.

"Oh Martha, what shall we do?" she wailed.

They were startled when a man's voice answered her.

"You must both come with me."

Scared, they sprang to their feet. They had thought they were alone.

"Who are you, sir?" Martha managed to stammer.

The man smiled. He had a gentle smile and the kindest brown eyes Rosie had ever seen. He was quite tall, and slim with light brown hair that fell loosely about his oval face which was beardless like

Veritan and Bellum. His clothes were simple, just a light grey tunic belted with leather, dark trousers and boots and a cloak of blue wool.

"I am Salvis," he told them. "I have heard of your trouble and I have come to help. Luke and Morwen are safe and I will take you to them, but the journey is long and already the first snow is starting to fall. We must leave now. Should Bellum's men find you, then you will surely die."

Rosie looked at Martha and back again to the stranger. Salvis placed a hand on each of their heads. Without words they both trusted him and a sense of peace gave them renewed strength.

Silently they followed him and did not look back.

Chapter 11

And dolphins race with rainbows

Food had never tasted so good. Taking a chunk of brown bread, Luke mopped the last of the broth from his dish and Morwen, sitting opposite him, did the same.

Kett's house was no more than a cave with a stone front built on to it, but it was warmed by a big log fire and kept dry with rush matting and hangings of wool and fur. The cave must have gone back a long way into the cliff, but the back was blocked off by a wall of timber, making the front into a room.

More importantly it was safe. Built halfway down the cliff on a wide ledge, it could only be reached by steps cut into the rock above and below, so that it was easy to defend and almost impossible to attack.

They felt safe here. Bellum would find it hard to reach them.

Kett was outside and from the small window they could see him walking along the rocky shore, his yellow head bent against the wind. He seemed to be watching for something, or someone.

"What is he waiting for?" Morwen whispered.

Luke shrugged and tore the last piece of bread in half so that they could share it.

"You can speak up, Morwen. He can't hear us

out there... I don't know what he's waiting for, but at least he took us in. D'you think we'll have to work hard?"

"Maybe. Already he has told you off for not calling him 'Master'. He wants us as servants, not friends."

Luke grinned. "So he did."

"Then you forgot again."

"So I did."

Morwen giggled. "You forgot on purpose, I feel?"

"I might have. Anyway, he's calling us to go outside. We'd better go."

Luke led the way down the narrow rock steps to the shore and they stood in front of Kett, both shivering. The sea breeze had become a strong wind and the sun was almost gone, leaving dark flurries of snow that stung their cheeks.

Kett was pointing down the beach.

"Strangers approaching. Are they known?"

Luke strained his sharp eyes against the fading light and could just make out three figures, a woman, a child and a man.

"Rosie!" he shouted. "Morwen, it's Rosie and your mother!"

"But that is not my father with them," Morwen said slowly. "That is not Tobias. That man is strong and tall."

"Who are these people?" Kett seemed anxious.

Morwen replied, "That is Luke's sister, Master Kett... and my mother... and I do not know the man."

"I do," Kett breathed. "Oh yes, yes, I do."

They spent a long time hugging each other and then slowly, falteringly, Rosie explained the dreadful thing that had happened to them.

"What of my father?" Morwen asked.

Martha sighed. "Oh Morwen, my daughter, Tobias is dead."

"No!" Morwen covered her face in her hands and burst into tears.

It was Luke who went to comfort her. For a few moments he forgot all about his own troubles and thought only of the pain she must feel.

When the tears had subsided, Luke remembered the other man and turned to look at him, standing patiently watching them.

Kett remembered him too.

"Sir," he said simply, "Tell me, are you the one who is to come?"

Salvis inclined his head. It was not a denial, but not an agreement either.

"I am Salvis. I want only to break Bellum's power."

"Then you are the one!"

Luke was staring at Salvis. "I know you... I've seen you before... at the King's Palace, you were there... only I couldn't exactly see you... but you were there."

Even to his own ears he did not make sense but Salvis agreed.

"Yes," he said. "I have always been here."

Suddenly Rosie squealed, making them all jump. "The dolphins are here! Telki and Praze, look!"

Wonderingly, they watched as the two dolphins came closer and closer to the shore, leaping and dancing through the water. Then they stood high in the waves and called to them.

"They are saying that all will be well for us," Morwen breathed. "I can sense it!"

Then, just as suddenly as they had come, the dolphins turned and, taking high leaps, headed out once more to the open sea. As they moved, they picked up the light of the sun through the snow and a whole rainbow of colour went with them.

"Oh look, look," Rosie gasped. "The dolphins are racing with rainbows!"

Luke's heart raced too.

'Where sea-birds fly from rocks of gold and dolphins race with rainbows...'

"It's Mummy's song," his sister breathed. "It's the song Mummy used to sing, but that's all I remember of it... This must be the place, Luke, the place where dolphins race with rainbows."

Luke said nothing. His mouth was too dry to speak. His heart was pounding and his teeth chattering.

Then he saw the miracle.

"Rosie, look at the sea!"

The mist had gone. On the far horizon they could see the cliffs of Cornwall. And tied to a nearby rock was their little rowing boat, complete with oars.

"That's right," Salvis said, very gently. "Now you can go home."

Kett had joined them at the water's edge. "You could go home. Or you could stay and fight. You could stay and help to take back the lost Kingdom. This is Salvis, the one we have been waiting for. The one who will win back Karensa for the King. He will need warriors in his army."

Salvis said seriously. "Think before you reply, both of you. If you stay you may never leave Karensa. You may die. Bellum will have no mercy. He will not treat you gently just because you are children."

Luke thought of Petroc, beaten and ill-treated by Carrik. He remembered how they had once walked in safety, where now they were scared to go. He thought of the Dark Forest, now taken over by Bellum's men. He thought of the King's kindness to them and he thought again of Petroc, who had promised to be his brother.

Rosie remembered Tobias, lying in his grave.

They looked at the boat, bobbing temptingly in the water.

Morwen started to cry again.

Luke and Rosie exchanged glances.

"Yes," Rosie murmured. "Yes Luke, we should stay."

"Are you sure?"

"I'm sure."

"Then we'll stay."

And with that, the mist returned over the sea.

Deep into the night they sat talking while the flames from the driftwood fire died and flared again as Kett instructed Luke to add more kindling. Morwen brewed tea from fragrant herbs and this warmed them while outside the snow fell in flurries, as if it could not quite make up its mind whether to snow or not.

It was hard to believe that after all these months they had given up their chance to go home. However, as Luke listened to Salvis talk, he knew that they had made the right decision.

There was something about Salvis that Luke did not understand. He could have listened to him all night, and very nearly did. He told them many things, secrets hidden since the beginning of time. Even Martha in her grief was still and quiet with Rosie snuggled beside her, almost asleep. Morwen looked very sad, but she was as eager as Luke to listen to Salvis.

Kett sat as one frozen in time. His bright, turquoise eyes never left Salvis for one moment.

"The Time of Snows is now here," Salvis told them. "Before the next Time of Plenty the Great Secret will be revealed, the secret promised for eternity. Then, the King's law will be restored."

"But that is so far away, Master," Morwen cried. "What of all those people Bellum will destroy before then? What of my brother, Petroc, forced to live with Bellum's men?"

"Petroc will come to no great harm," Salvis said gently.

"But Master... he... he is not treated well... Already my father has died... Don't let it be my brother too..."

A tear rolled down her cheek. Luke felt something deep inside himself begin to ache for the hurt that she felt. He would like to have taken her hand, but he was too embarrassed.

"We'll rescue him, Morwen. We have to," he said. Salvis said nothing.

Kett leant forward and stirred the dying flames with an iron rod. Sparks flew in all directions as the driftwood spluttered.

"This is the boy with Carrik?" he asked slowly.

Luke nodded. "He didn't want to go. He didn't have any choice. They made him."

"Well... tomorrow morning at dawn, Carrik is to move his entire household to Bellum's stronghold for the Time of Snows. To make that journey they must pass through the Dark Forest and go a certain way, a way known to me. Deep in the forest is a river which they must cross at the shallow part which is used as a ford. Right now the water is swollen and they will have to stop to help the horses cross with the heavy carts... maybe, at this ford, we could steal Petroc away from them..."

Chapter 12

One less, one more

A thin layer of snow sparkled in the morning sunlight. Every branch of every tree, every bush, every blade of grass was edged with silvery white.

It was very cold. As they moved deeper and deeper into the Dark Forest, the sun disappeared, to be replaced by sullen grey skies that threatened more snow would come soon.

Kett and Luke walked in silence. Kett had given Luke a cloak of fur and he tried to keep his hands hidden beneath it to stop them from turning blue with cold.

Luke was scared and excited at the same time; thrilled by the danger and excited that tonight he could be sharing his supper with Petroc, but fearful that they might fail. Kett had warned him of the risk as they had made plans last night and Luke knew that this strange, wild-looking man was also afraid.

Kett stopped abruptly and drew Luke back with him.

"We are close to the ford where Carrik will have to slow down. I know a place we may hide where none shall ever find us... Come..."

As they left the track, the ground fell away steeply and in one place formed an overhanging cave, completely hidden by dense undergrowth.

They could see everything but not be seen.

"This is great," Luke breathed. "At home we..." He stopped, his voice trailing away into silence.

At home they would have made a den and played games. But this was no game. This was for real.

He was surprised when Kett laughed. "Stay brave, Luke. You have been brave so far. Do not falter now. Listen, Carrik's men are coming. When they are here, when it is time for us to act, then the fear will go. This is the hardest part, waiting and wondering. This is the time when courage deserts us."

Kett must have had sharp ears for Luke could not hear anything at all, but soon he also picked up the sound which could only be that of a great household on the move.

He closed his mouth tightly to stop his teeth from chattering. He wished Salvis or even the girls were here, but the mission was thought to be too dangerous to risk Salvis being captured, and the girls would be sure to slow them down.

Even that time at home when Luke had stolen a car radio for a dare had not felt as frightened as this. If he had been caught then he would have been up before a magistrate... If he was caught now he might be locked away... or worse...

He had to take the risk for Petroc's sake. Kett put a reassuring hand on his shoulder; he seemed to understand.

Carrik moved slowly, hampered by awkward carts that slid across the frosty ground, not always in the direction he wanted them to go.

The landlord himself was leading the way,

followed by his own servants and then the carts loaded with goods that he had probably stolen from people still loyal to the King.

Right at the back, on his own, was Petroc. To make sure he did not escape, Carrik had tied his hands to the back of the cart he was following.

For a little while, anger drove Luke's fear away. It seemed as though all the life had been taken from his friend. He walked with bowed shoulders; he had been so strong, but now he stumbled over the uneven ground. Even his bright red hair seemed dull and he stared ahead looking neither to left nor right.

Just as Kett had predicted, the procession stopped at the ford.

Kett grinned. His eyes were bright with excitement. Now he seemed to be enjoying himself.

"Things could not be better," he breathed. "The boy is quite alone. They have either forgotten about him or they are certain he cannot escape."

"Won't they come for him to help them through the water?" Luke whispered back.

"No. They'll not risk him escaping into the forest." Kett pulled a hunting dagger from his belt. "Come boy, you keep him quiet. I'll cut him free."

Luke froze, suddenly scared again.

"This is the only chance we shall get," Kett urged.

Life returned to Luke's body. Stealthily they crept up behind Petroc who still stared ahead as if half asleep. Luke sprang on him, covering his friend's mouth with his hand.

He expected a struggle but Petroc had no strength left.

"Petroc... Petroc, it's me... Luke! We've come for you!"

He felt the older boy relax in his grip and took his hand away from his mouth.

Petroc turned to face him. "Luke... it is really you!"

"Be quiet, talk later," Kett ordered tersely. He slashed at the ropes with his dagger and suddenly Petroc was free.

Kett pulled them away. "We must hide. We'll not have time to run. They are sure to notice the boy is missing before they reach Bellum's stronghold."

The three of them raced towards the hidden cave and that was when things started to go wrong.

Kett slipped on the ice and fell heavily. He sat on the ground, his face white with pain, holding his ankle. His foot pointed out at a strange angle.

At the same time a cry from one of Carrik's men warned them that they had heard.

"Quickly Kett, get up... We'll help you!" Luke gasped.

Kett shook his head. "It is too late for me, Luke. My time is finished. Something told me when we set out that I would not be going back. Now the hour belongs to Salvis and he will call men to his side in a way that I cannot. One must grow less, one more. It is the way it has to be... you two must run and make sure that Carrik's men do not see you."

Luke and Petroc exchanged glances, then Luke nodded.

"No sense in us all being taken," he said. But before they left Kett to his fate, Luke bent down and took his hand.

"Thank you, Master," he said simply.

Kett nodded, accepting the boy's acknowledgement of respect, but he repeated that they must go.

That was when the second thing went wrong. As they leapt wildly into the cave, Luke misjudged his distance and caught his shoulder on a jagged branch. It tore his arm and even as he watched, his tunic turned red with blood.

He felt no pain, only surprise, but Petroc looked horrified.

"It's not that bad," Luke insisted. "Really, it looks worse than it is."

"It does not, it needs binding up... Luke, I'm going back to Carrik."

Luke gasped. "You can't!"

"Yes I can... Luke we are promised as brothers. If I go back, Carrik will not look for you. If I stay here he will search and find us both."

"No... no, Petroc... please, don't do this!"

But Petroc had already gone. Carrik's men saw him and lost no time in securing him to the cart again. They had tossed Kett in too, and he lay helpless, his broken ankle preventing him from getting away. They obviously thought that he alone was responsible for Petroc's escape.

Then they moved on.

Quietly, Luke began to cry. There in the woodland cave he cried for Petroc and for Kett, for himself, for Tobias and even for the King in his Palace and for his dad waiting at home. When he was through with that he cried for his mother for the very first time. Seemingly, neither the sky above nor the ground below nor the forest creatures around him, cared.

He never knew how long he lay there, but when he

felt safe to move it had begun to snow again, not flurries this time but a serious blizzard.

Now his shoulder and arm had started to hurt and the wound was still oozing blood. He felt horribly cold. He wrapped his cloak tightly around his arm to try to stop the bleeding and started to make his way back to the only place he could go: Kett's house.

As he stumbled along he left a trail of red in the snow which any could have followed. However new snow was falling so fast that his tracks were instantly covered and the remaining traces could easily have been left by a wounded animal.

It was strange, but he felt at peace, as though his tears had washed away his hurts, at least for the time being.

He came to the edge of the Dark Forest and began to follow the cliff path back towards the Bay of Dolphins, then he rounded a bend and saw a dark shape in front of him through the snow.

His head was spinning. He thought he was back in the sea being rescued by Telki and Praze, the dolphins.

It was Salvis, himself, who scooped him up in his strong arms and carried him to safety.

Chapter 13

The Bay of Peace

Luke was comfortable and very warm. He was aware of soft furs around him, a blazing fire and people watching him. He could hear the sea crashing on the rocks in the distance. He opened his eyes and Salvis was looking down at him.

"Rest, Luke, while you can. Allow your strength to return to you."

As he struggled to wake up, Luke remembered Kett and Petroc and the blizzard. He looked beneath the fur covering him at his shoulder. It was clean and bandaged.

Someone put a beaker of yellow liquid in his hands. Suddenly curious, he stared down at it and asked, "What is this stuff?"

"You would call it medicine," Salvis replied. "It is only for those in need and you have a need, Luke, so drink it."

Luke obeyed and at once felt the strength returning to his body. He sat up and looked around. He was back in Kett's house. Martha, Morwen and Rosie were all staring at him.

Feeling self-conscious he began to say, "What's the matter?" then he caught sight of two other people in the room. "Josh! Delfi! What are you doing here? Salvis... Salvis, we lost Petroc... and Kett, Kett was taken too."

He was surprised when Salvis calmly nodded. "Kett's hour is over. And do not concern yourself about Petroc for he will come to no real harm. His heart will always remain loyal to the King."

"But what about the rest of him?" Luke cried.

"The rest of him too," Salvis said, smiling gently.

Morwen came over and pressed his arm, the good one that had not been hurt.

"At least you tried, Luke," she said bravely. "Petroc now knows that we have not forgotten him."

"You must take time to get well," Martha added. "After all, I shall not prosper by losing both of my sons."

Luke closed his eyes, suddenly tired. He had failed. He had cost Kett his freedom, maybe even his life. Petroc was back in Bellum's stronghold, yet his mother and sister had no reproach, only kindness.

He slept. Later, much later, he learnt that Josh and Delfi had joined Salvis after their supplies of food had run out and Delfi's mother had died of a terrible fever. Delfi had not spoken a single word since her mother's death. Her sorrow had taken the power of speech away from her. Once Josh would have been able to go to the King's Palace for food and medicine, but that was no longer possible.

The Time of Snows was well named. Snow fell in droves, drifted, froze and then fell again. The sky always seemed grey and heavy with the promise of more snow to come and it was so cold, colder than Luke and Rosie could ever remember at home. Only the Bay of Dolphins was clear, for the salt from the sea melted the snow as fast as it fell.

During this time many people came to the Bay of Dolphins to join Salvis; broken, hurting people who found that simply being with Salvis seemed to bring healing into their lives. They made homes for themselves in the many caves in the cliffs. Soon they were ready to fight and die to defeat Bellum and restore the Lost Kingdom. They only lacked one thing. They had courage, they had purpose, but they had no weapons and Salvis did not seem to think weapons were important.

"Bellum must be defeated without swords," he told them, over and over again.

None argued with Salvis. His authority was never questioned and the peace that came from him was passed on to all who came to him. Soon the Bay of Dolphins was re-named the Bay of Peace.

Luke and Rosie, Morwen, Martha and Salvis shared Kett's house. They ate simply from Kett's store and they slept on straw and furs, yet Luke found a contentment he had never known before. The Time of Snows was the most uncomfortable and yet the happiest he had ever known.

Often he would sit with Rosie and Morwen and listen while Salvis told them stories that for some reason seemed familiar. He would talk to Luke and Rosie as if he knew all about their world.

The children loved these times. They had never met anyone like Salvis before.

One day, Rosie and Delfi were building a snow-house. Luke and Morwen had gone off on their own again. Rosie had found a friend in Delfi; she was good company, she had a great sense of fun and could make herself understood quite well without using words.

"This is how eskimos live, it's an igloo," Rosie was explaining as they worked, patting the huge ice blocks into a circle.

Delfi laughed and pointed to a gap in the wall.

"Well, eskimos are better at building than me."

Delfi shrugged questioningly.

"Oh... eskimos... they live in my world, Delfi, at a place called the North Pole...or is it the South Pole? Anyway it's very cold and the only thing they have to build houses from is snow."

As the igloo took shape, Salvis joined them and with his help they did manage to construct something that looked like a snow-house.

"This will be here until the Time of Snows passes," Salvis told them as he put the last block of ice in place. Like the girls, his face was red with cold and exertion.

"What comes after the Time of Snows?" Rosie asked.

"The Time of New Birth and after that the Time of Plenty... the best time on Karensa... only I shall not be with you then..."

Salvis suddenly looked sad and Delfi threw her arms about his knees, shaking her head from side to side.

Salvis pulled away. "Child, don't you ever want to speak?"

She nodded.

Salvis placed a finger on her lips. "Then you will speak," he promised, as Rosie stared in disbelief.

That evening they all sat together by the fire. Josh and Delfi had joined them for supper and they had eaten well of fresh fish, new bread and vegetables.

Luke and Morwen sat close together. Rosie tried to see if they were holding hands, but couldn't quite tell. In recent days when she spoke of Morwen to Luke his face turned pink. Sometimes she did it on purpose to see what would happen.

"Delfi, will you play for us?" Salvis asked.

Delfi took up her lyre and began to play softly, a haunting melody, so sad it made them all think of homes and families they had lost.

Salvis asked if she knew the words of the song.

Delfi nodded.

"Will you sing them for us then?"

A hush fell over them all. Breaking through the silence, Delfi began to sing.

"There is a land for broken dreams,
A place the aching heart knows,
Where sea birds fly from rocks of gold
And dolphins race with rainbows.

Where woodland creatures freely roam
The healing stream of peace flows.
Release your heart to find that place
Where dolphins race with rainbows."

There was a pause. "I can speak again," she whispered.

Josh gave a cry and swept her into his arms.

Rosie gasped. "That's my mother's song! Luke, that's the song she used to sing! I remember!" and she burst into tears.

Luke felt his own eyes fill with tears.

Through it all, Salvis stayed calm, but Luke looked up at him in wonder.

"Who are you, Salvis? Who are you really?"

"Who do you say I am?"

"I don't know... I think... I don't know..."

"You will know. Before you leave Karensa you will know for sure."

News of Delfi's healing travelled fast and many more came to Salvis. Some were made well; some were not. Some went back to their homes; others stayed and added to their number.

Bad news came as well. Bellum had executed Kett. When Salvis was told of this he went to the beach and sat for a long time by himself, oblivious to the cold, just looking far out to sea.

When he returned to the house he took Luke and Rosie to one side.

"The time for preparation is nearly over," he said. "Soon the snows will melt and, before the Time of Plenty comes, Bellum must be defeated. You two have come to Karensa for a reason for you have a part to play, but first of all we must go to the King's Palace for his blessing. When the dolphins return to the bay we shall make our move."

Later that day Luke sat outside and looked out over the bay. The cold was not so fierce now and here and there a few blades of grass could be seen through the snow.

Morwen joined him. Since they had been with Salvis, Luke and Morwen had become very close. She had become his sister as Petroc was his brother.

Yet she was more than a sister now.

She had unbraided her hair and it fell in red-gold clouds about her shoulders. Her green eyes were sad.

"What are you thinking of, Luke?" she murmured.

"Oh... things... home... and Petroc."

"I, too think of Petroc," she admitted. "Yet Salvis promised he would be safe and I do trust Salvis."

"Salvis seems very sad lately... Morwen, who do you think he really is?"

She paused. "He must be a Lord of the Palace, like Veritan, like Bellum was before he... before..."

"No, he's more than that... When Rosie and I went to the King's Palace, I'm sure Salvis was there, only we couldn't see him... I think Salvis must be the King's Son."

Before the words had left his mouth, they saw a movement in the water. At the same moment the sun came out and in a rainbow of cascading light, two dolphins raced across the bay.

"The dolphins are home," Luke said simply. "It is time for us to go."

Chapter 14

The greatest King of all

One morning just after the Time of Snows had ended, and the island of Karensa was once again clothed in green, Salvis told Luke and Rosie that it was time for them to go to the King's Palace. They were both excited and scared for the journey was to be full of danger.

The land between the Bay of Dolphins and the Royal Palace would be well guarded by Lord Bellum's men. Bellum hated Salvis, but even he would not dare to invade the Bay of Dolphins with its steep cliffs and many caves, all occupied by Salvis' people.

Out in the Dark Forest it would be easy for Bellum or Carrik or any of their servants to capture them. Once they were in Bellum's stronghold they might never see freedom again.

"There's just one thing, Salvis," Luke said as they prepared to go. "Why us?" It was a question that had been niggling him for some time. "Why not take two strong men who could defend you? Me and Rosie, we're not yet grown."

"I will take who I will take," Salvis replied in a quiet voice. "You have a part to play in this. You are all the defence I shall need. You did not come to Karensa by chance. The King sent Telki and Praze to save you from the sea. In the months you have been here you have been changing and growing and preparing for this time."

Rosie glanced sideways at her brother. Salvis' words gave her a thrill of excitement, even though she was scared. And it was true, Luke had changed. He looked like any other island boy now. His fair hair had grown long to his shoulders and he had become muscular and weather-beaten from spending so much time in the open air. For much of the time he even spoke as an islander. But the biggest change was that he no longer lost his temper when things did not go his way. There was a peace about him that must have come from Salvis. Luke was the strong, brave older brother she had always longed for.

What Rosie did not realise was that this same peace surrounded her, too. Sometimes she would find herself singing lines from Delfi's song.

"Where woodland creatures freely roam, the healing stream of peace flows..."

The stream of peace did not come from Karensa. It came from Salvis himself.

"Aren't we going to take any weapons?" Luke was asking. They were standing in the doorway of Kett's house saying goodbye to the others.

Josh produced a small dagger.

"Take this, Salvis. It will provide protection should you meet Lord Bellum's men."

"And I have a fishing knife for Luke," Delfi added softly, making signs as she held out the bone handled tool. She was not yet used to being able to speak again.

But Salvis brushed them aside. "We will do better without weapons. My time is not yet come to destroy Bellum. For today we shall be safe."

Luke was surprised to see Josh's eyes darken with anger, and he watched the fisherman turn away abruptly. When he turned back he seemed as normal, but that brief moment had made Luke feel uncomfortable. He did not know why.

Martha came out carrying a parcel. "At least take bread and cheese with you for the journey?"

Rosie looked up at the plump, now grey haired woman who had taken them in and treated them as her own children. Martha missed Tobias still. Often she would be found with her eyes red from crying, yet there was never a complaint, never a word of reproach. Rosie felt a sudden rush of love for her.

"Thank you, Martha. Oh, I do love you so!" she cried and was rewarded by a hug from Martha and a big smile of approval from Salvis.

"Come now," their leader said. "The Palace is a long way."

He did not need to add that it was a way fraught with danger.

The morning air was fresh and the grassy banks bright with flowers of yellow, blue and pink. Birds sang from trees bursting with white blossom and small creatures scuttled busily through the long grass – the Time of New Birth on Karensa.

As they turned from the sea towards the Dark Forest they caught sight of two dolphins leaping above the waves in a spray of sparkling rainbow light.

Once more Telki and Praze were racing with rainbows.

Lord Bellum was waiting for them not far from the place where they had tried to rescue Petroc and, even in their fear, they knew that Bellum was magnificent to look upon.

Seated on the same horse that had once carried Luke to the Royal Palace, dressed now in black and silver, his dark hair covered by a plumed helmet, he appeared so much bigger than when Luke and Rosie had first seen him.

Close behind him, also on horseback, were two servants, each richly dressed and wearing the sign of the serpent on their tabards.

Luke tried to stop his knees from shaking, but Rosie was trembling. Salvis placed a hand on each of their shoulders and whispered to them, "Don't worry. We shall not be hurt."

At once they stopped shaking and some of their courage returned.

Slowly, lazily, Lord Bellum slid from his horse and stood before them, a huge figure emanating darkness.

"Well, Salvis, here you are," he breathed in a low, musical voice, soft and mocking.

"Here I am Bellum," Salvis replied steadily. "But where are you?"

"Me?" Bellum gave a short laugh. "I know where I am, Salvis. I am here waiting to do battle, and then I shall take my rightful place as ruler of Karensa."

For the first time ever, Salvis grew angry. "That you will never do, Bellum. The rightful ruler of Karensa is the King!"

"The people do not say it!"

"Many still do. And those that do not are wrong. It will not be long before the way to the King's

Palace is open again to all. Until then, Bellum, stand back and let us pass."

"Until then, Salvis... until then go with your friends from the world.... Make the most of the time you have before we meet in battle and I destroy you... Until then..."

He and his men drew aside so that they could walk by. As Luke brushed past Bellum, the Lord hissed in his ear.

"You are on the wrong side, boy. Join me and you shall see your friend Petroc set free."

Luke looked straight ahead and pretended not to hear, although his heart was pounding.

"That was scary," Rosie whispered when they were safely out of earshot.

"Yes it was," Salvis agreed, "And you were both very brave."

Luke said nothing. He felt as though he had just witnessed two giants in conflict, one evil and one good.

There was going to be a battle and Salvis was sure he would win. Yet Lord Bellum felt equally certain of his own victory.

The King's Palace did not seem to have changed; once inside it still shone with the same silver light. The jewels in the King's crown still reflected all the colours of the rainbow onto the floor.

But this time they were greeted with a fanfare of trumpets and, as they walked slowly towards the King's throne, every knee bowed before them. Luke knew that it was Salvis they honoured. Even Lord Veritan knelt and bowed his silver head to the ground.

Luke and Rosie looked around, once again completely in awe of their surroundings. Luke realised that two things had changed. No line of people awaited the King's judgement, for Bellum had stopped anyone from drawing near to the King. And the other thing that was missing was Bellum's throne. He would not be needing it any more.

Salvis stood before the King's throne and bowed low and it seemed natural for the children to fall to their knees.

"The time has come, Lord King," Salvis said, and there was sorrow in his voice.

The King sighed deeply, but when he spoke his voice still rang with the power of creation.

"You are right, Salvis, the time has come. It will be hard for you to bear. Are you prepared?"

"Lord King, I am prepared... only... my heart is heavy... Can there be no other way?"

The King spoke gently. "There is no other way, Salvis. If there were, I would not ask you to do this. This is written in the ancient Law of Creation. You are the only one with the power to defeat Bellum... Yes, it is hard, but it is the only way. It is the way I would have you go."

Veritan rose to his feet and drew his great sword from its scabbard. The blade flashed golden bright.

"Lord King," he said. "This sword has always fought for truth and has never yet been defeated. I give it freely to Salvis!"

"No, no, Veritan my faithful friend." Once again the King sighed deeply and the sigh echoed around the Palace so that it seemed as if the whole of Karensa sighed with him. "Such a weapon will not defeat the Lord of Darkness. Only the truth of my word which is written in Salvis' heart can bring Bellum down and restore my Kingdom."

Slowly Veritan replaced the sword in its scabbard.

"Lord King, if you would send Salvis to do this, you must love your people very much."

"Oh yes," the King whispered. "I love my people more than they will ever know... Now, you have brought the children to me as I asked. Let them come closer."

Luke and Rosie got to their feet and stood one on either side of the King's throne. Rosie was crying softly, but Luke was past tears. The sorrow of the day had become so real to him that he could not cry. Neither of them understood what was happening, only that here was deep love and that this must be the greatest King of all.

"Well, Luke, Rosie, you do not look much like the two children that came to me from the sea, only half-dressed as I recall. One is no longer a child and will be called to play a man's part in what is to come... Luke, you have grown in stature and in spirit. Have you learnt from Karensa?"

"Yes, Lord King," Luke replied truthfully.

"Really learnt?"

"Yes, Lord King," Luke said firmly. "I've learnt to... to put other people before my own needs... and to be loyal... and, I think, brave..."

"Then you have only one more thing to learn and that you will do before you return to Poldawn... Now Rosie, what have you learnt?"

Rosie hesitated and the King did not hurry her. Finally she said, "I've learnt to stand up for what I believe in... and... to love people, even though they might not love me."

"Then you too have learnt well. Now kneel, all of you. My desire is to bless you before you leave."

As they knelt quietly before this great King, it seemed as though time stood still and everyone else in the great hall had disappeared. It was just Salvis, Luke and Rosie kneeling before the King's throne.

The King placed his hands on each head in turn and as he did so he spoke to each of them.

"Luke, my brave warrior, when you return to your world you will have great work to do. Learn your last lesson well, my child. Nurture it in your heart... Rosie, your gentle nature holds strength and courage that will surprise many... Salvis," the King's voice trembled, "Ah, Salvis, my own dear son, if there were any other way I would take this from you, but there is not... My son you are as dear to me as my own life, no even more dear. I know that your love for me is such that you will obey me though it will cost you everything..."

Then he told them to rise.

"The time is at hand. Go now. You are prepared."

Chapter 15

Ready for battle

"Are you afraid?" Morwen asked.

The three of them, Morwen, Luke and Rosie, were sitting in front of Salvis' army which was camped on the far side of the Dark Forest. Before them was a wide, shallow valley, green and strewn with wild flowers. The valley was fed by a clear stream, the same stream that ran through the forest and emptied into the sea just beyond the Bay of Dolphins. On the other side of the valley stood Bellum's stronghold which was a massive, fort-like structure with high walls.

They had moved from the Bay of Dolphins at dawn and it had taken all day to reach this place. Many were still loyal to the King and all who could walk, except a few women and the young children, had come to help Salvis take back the land which Bellum had stolen.

They made a strange army: the lame who had been healed, the poor, the desperate, the homeless, all those to whom Salvis had given hope.

Now it was dark. They had eaten together and were ready to fight, to take by storm that stronghold that seemed to brood evil.

From where they sat they could hear Bellum's men laughing and singing; the sound drifted over the valley on the warm night air.

They sat quietly and waited for the dawn. Salvis made no speech to give them heart for the battle. Instead he went from one group to the other, encouraging them in the way they most needed to hear.

"I'm scared. Even though the King gave us his blessing, I'm still scared," Rosie admitted.

She was, too. Her teeth were chattering.

After a while Luke agreed. This was not the time to boast or tell lies.

"I'm afraid," he said. "Maybe... maybe real courage is to fight when you're still afraid?"

"Do you wish you'd never come to Karensa?" Morwen asked suddenly.

Luke thought about that. If he hadn't argued over a bowl of cornflakes, if he hadn't taken the boat out too far from shore, they would be safe at home with Dad and Stacey.

He would never have met Petroc or Tobias or Martha or Morwen... He had grown close to Morwen. She was special to him. And he would not have met Salvis.

"I don't wish that, Morwen. I believe that our visit to Karensa was meant to be. That's what the King said." Rosie answered for him.

This was the place where Luke had grown up. It was the place Mum had sung about, the place of peace.

"No," he said firmly. "I don't ever regret coming here."

"What if... tomorrow, what if..."

"What if I should be killed?"

Morwen nodded miserably. A big tear rolled down her cheek.

Luke took her hands in his own. His were large and brown. Hers were small and thin. He could easily have crushed them in his own.

"If I die, then it will be for the greatest man ever."

"Salvis?"

"Lord Salvis, the King's own son... I don't want to die. I want to live and see the King's land restored to him, but I'd follow Salvis to the ends of the earth."

"I think we have," said Rosie.

They were quiet, then Morwen said, "Where is Salvis?"

Luke got to his feet and scanned the encamped army.

"He's still talking to people. There are so many of them, hundreds and hundreds, far more than Bellum's men."

"Yes, but," Rosie bit her lip.

"But what?"

"But... I know Salvis said we were not to look for weapons but... Bellum's men have swords and axes and spears. How are we going to fight them? We only have a few fishing knives and daggers between us."

It was the question that was uppermost in Luke's mind. He knew he should trust Salvis and the King, but just how were they going to do battle?

Lord Bellum was not likely to simply give in to their demands. He would fight to the death to see that Karensa stayed in his hands.

Luke wanted to fight. He wanted a sword and a shield. The King had called him a brave warrior and he wanted to be one.

Besides, if he was not to fight what was the special work that the King had given to him?

Morwen sighed. "We need to trust the King... But it is hard."

Salvis came over to them at last and sat down with them on the grass.

"This is the testing time," he said simply, speaking to them now as if they were already grown-up. "You have been faithful to the King. Will you stay faithful even now?"

Morwen looked down at the grass. "I want to. But Salvis, I'm afraid."

Luke put his arm about her shoulder. He wanted to keep her from this, but he knew it was the last thing she would have wanted. Her brother was in Bellum's stronghold and Morwen wanted to set him free.

"I'm afraid too," Rosie whispered and Luke gave her a hug with his free arm. Surely Salvis did not expect one as young as Rosie to fight with him?

"What about you, Luke?" Salvis said in a low voice. "Will you stay faithful to the end?"

Luke felt his face turn red, that Salvis should need to ask such a question.

"Salvis, you know I will!"

Salvis smiled at him, but when Luke met his gaze he saw that Lord Salvis' dark eyes were heavy with sorrow.

"Come then my children, we must go. Morwen, you must find Delfi, the daughter of Josh and look after her."

"Where's Josh? I want to come with you!"

"Josh... Josh has been... called away. Delfi needs

you, Morwen."

"Let her stay with Martha then. Salvis, I must come with you! I must find Petroc!"

"That is not your task. Morwen, Delfi needs you. She will need your comfort very soon. You must take care of her. You will understand in time. Luke, Rosie, will you come a little further with me?"

Morwen looked crestfallen but reluctantly she obeyed and turned away, giving Luke and Rosie a hug before she left them. She was too upset to speak.

When she had gone Luke said, "She wanted to come with us, Salvis."

"Well, she could not," Salvis replied sternly. "The first rule about fighting in a battle, Luke, is that you obey orders. Now, come with me. Time is short. This must be done before break of day."

They stopped by the stream and sat down on a grassy bank. It was a peaceful spot, in spite of the sounds of Bellum's army, louder now that they were nearer to his stronghold.

Salvis seemed more distressed than ever.

Tentatively Rosie stretched out her hand.

"Salvis, we won't leave you. All your people are ready to fight. You won't be alone."

There were tears on Salvis' face. "Rosie, Luke, before dawn every one of these will desert me. This battle I have to fight alone."

Luke thought he meant a duel between himself and Bellum.

"But you can't!" he cried. "Bellum is not to be trusted. He'll trick you!"

"I must fight alone," Salvis insisted.

Luke and Rosie looked at each other in amazement. Neither of them had ever even thought Salvis meant to do this.

While they were still puzzling about it, Salvis said, "See, they are coming for me now."

Rosie clung to her brother. Coming from the stronghold was a band of armed men, carrying torches and swords.

Suddenly Luke gave a shout. "It's all right! Josh is with them! Look, it's Josh! Don't you recognise him? He must have got some of Bellum's men on our side. It's going to be all right. Josh, Josh, it's us!"

Josh did not call back to him. The band of men stopped in front of them, looking at Salvis as if they dared not go any further.

"That's the one," Josh said at last. "Yes, that's the man you want."

Immediately the men moved forward and seized Salvis, binding him with strong ropes. Salvis did not resist. It was Luke who sprang forward to defend him, but he stood no chance against grown men and both he and Rosie were held fast.

To Luke's horror, Carrik moved forward from the back of the men.

"Take them too," he said. "They chose to follow Salvis, they can die with him!"

"No!" Josh intervened. "You have the man you wanted. I have served you well. Let me have the children. They are friends of my girl and it would hurt her to see them come to any harm. I will see they are kept safe until Bellum is seated in the King's Palace."

Carrik gave a short laugh. "So be it. Take men with you and make them safe."

Luke struggled as hard as he could to get free, but he was held in a grip of steel by two of Bellum's men. All his struggles gained him was more pain.

Josh led the way as they were forced up the valley to a round hut built of rough stone.

"A woodman's hut," Josh explained. "We'll leave them here until it is accomplished, then they will have to do as we say."

Roughly they were thrown inside onto the hard floor. Before they left Josh turned to them.

"Salvis could never win! A battle without weapons, what battle is that? Don't you see?"

"I saw Salvis healing Delfi!" Luke cried. "How could you betray him after that? How could you, Josh?"

Josh's answer was to slam the door shut and put the heavy iron bar in place.

They were alone in the dark and they knew that there was no escape.

"What's going to happen to us, Luke?" Rosie whispered.

"I don't know. What's more important, what's going to happen to Salvis? What are they doing to him right now?"

Chapter 16

Bellum's stronghold

Luke gave the door a final kick.

"It's no use, Rosie, it won't move. We'll never escape!"

By now their eyes had become accustomed to the dark so that they were able to discern vague outlines. They could see each other. They had found a pile of split logs when Luke had tripped over them trying to find his way about.

They had located the door by the gap between door and wall but as yet it was still too dark outside to be of any help to them at all.

Rosie sat down on the log pile and put her head in her hands.

"What are we going to do, Luke?" she said hopelessly.

"I don't know. It's all gone wrong."

"Why didn't Salvis fight?"

"I don't know."

"Why did Josh betray him?"

"Rosie!" Luke's voice rose in desperation. "I don't know, I don't know!"

He was sorry then. It was hardly Rosie's fault, after all. "I'm sorry, Rosie. I didn't mean to shout at you, but... but I just don't know, that's all... If only Salvis had..."

"Ssh! Ssh, listen, Luke!"

The noise came again only the door was so thick that they could hardly hear it, but someone was lifting the bar from the outside. Luke's heart was thumping so loudly he thought that Rosie must hear it. Surely Josh's men had not come for them already? He had not said so to Rosie, but he knew that they would never be set free. Carrik would not risk them helping Salvis' men.

As they clung together the door creaked open. They gasped. In the darkness of early morning stood... Morwen.

The sudden relief of being rescued made Luke forget himself completely and he threw his arms round Morwen and held her tightly. Then, realising what he was doing he pulled away and gave Rosie a much-needed hug, too.

"Morwen, what do you think you're doing here?" he asked and even to his own ears that sounded ungracious.

"I followed you." Morwen sounded quite proud of herself. "I followed you all the way from the camp. I was just waiting for Josh and Carrik to go before I could set you free... They took ages... They... they were making sport with Salvis... it was horrible..."

"Where's Delfi?"

"With Martha, back at Kett's house. Martha is looking after all the young children."

"You disobeyed Salvis," Luke said sternly. "Salvis told you to take care of Delfi."

"She's better off with Martha. And I'm glad I didn't obey Salvis or you would still be shut up in that woodman's hut!" She tossed back her long red plaits in a defiant gesture. "If you had not obeyed him, he might still be free."

"Oh, stop it both of you!" shouted Rosie, putting her hands over her ears. "Stop arguing! Stop shouting! We have to return to the camp and get help. We have to get Salvis away from Bellum before it's too late!"

"She's right," Luke said. "You two must run like the wind and tell them. Run as you have never run before. Tell them to bring what weapons they have and come prepared to fight to set Salvis free."

"They won't listen to us," Morwen argued. "And anyway, what are you going to do?"

"I shall go to Bellum's stronghold."

Rosie gasped in dismay. "Oh Luke, you can't!"

"Yes I can. Bellum won't do anything to me immediately, or to Salvis. He'll want to have some fun first. That should give you two time to get the men together. I know many of them have got swords hidden away in spite of everything they were told about not needing them. And daggers. And staves. Even fishing knives. Bring whatever they have but don't waste any time."

"But I want to go with you. I want to find Petroc. And the men will not listen to me."

"Yes they will," Luke insisted. "You're the one person they will listen to. Your father, Tobias, was well respected by all for the way he lost his life for the King."

For a moment it seemed as though she would argue again, but then she gave in.

"Morwen," said Rosie, "Delfi... don't... I mean..."

"She will have to know what Josh has done, Rosie," Morwen said very gently. "But yes, we must be careful not to hurt her any more than we need. And Luke... oh Luke, please be careful. Be very careful."

Then, to his astonishment, and embarrassment, she placed a kiss on his cheek.

Luke watched them go and then resolutely turned towards the place he most feared: Bellum's stronghold.

What remained of the night became his friend for it cloaked him as he sped across the valley.

Soon enough the great fortress loomed above him. He flattened himself against the high wall, and listened to the clamour that came from inside. Flickering torches lit the sky as the shouts of rejoicing added to Luke's fear. The cry was unmistakeable. They were calling for Salvis to die.

The two guards on the gate were joining in, neglecting their watch and turning their backs to the entrance that they were meant to be guarding, in order to see what was going on inside.

Luke seized his chance. Swiftly, silently, he crept along the side of the wall, his body pressed hard against its wooden stakes, until he reached the gateway. It was unbarred. It was easy then to crawl behind the two men and pass through into the stronghold.

He looked around. He found himself in an open courtyard in the centre of which stood a high platform lit by many torches. Standing on the platform were two men: Bellum and Salvis. In the torchlight Bellum seemed stronger than ever, his head thrown back in laughter as, with his sword held high in the air, he encouraged the people to call for Salvis' death.

Salvis faced him silently, his face bruised and bloodstained. He offered no resistance. He said nothing, only gazed steadily at the Lord of the Palace who had once been his father's, the King's, friend.

For a split second, it seemed to Luke almost as if Salvis was the victor and Bellum defeated. Part of him wanted to leap up to the platform and free Salvis, but his feet were rooted to the ground. Even when Bellum struck Salvis with his sword, so that he fell down, Luke could not move.

"You're one of Salvis' followers!"

Luke started. By his side stood a servant girl of about his own age.

"I'm not!" he shouted. "You must be thinking of someone else!"

"No... it was you. I saw you once leaving the Bay of Dolphins. You're the boy the dolphins brought in from the storm."

"Not me!"

"Well you must have a twin brother who looks just like you!"

Angrily, Luke turned on her. "Look, how many more times, it was not me! I don't know this Salvis and I don't want to know him either!"

She shrugged. "It doesn't matter now. He's going to die."

Scared and ashamed, Luke crept back towards the gate and tonight it was as easy to slip out of Bellum's stronghold as it was to get in.

Once outside he ran blindly, trying to blot out the memory of what he had done. Then, when he could run no more, at the very spot where they had taken Salvis, he threw himself down in the long grass, shivering and waiting for the release of tears.

But no tears came.

Morwen and Rosie found him there and between them they pulled him to his feet. Both girls were distressed.

"The army's gone, Luke!" Rosie told him. "Our army, once they found that Salvis had been taken, wouldn't fight. They turned and went home!"

Morwen added, "They left Salvis when he needed them most." She seemed unable to understand.

Luke groaned. "Why tell me? I'm as bad."

"But you went after him!" Morwen protested.

"Yes, but I left him. I pretended I didn't know him. I ran away!"

The girls stared at him, not knowing what to say. Then, suddenly, Morwen pointed across the valley. A figure was coming towards them, a familiar figure they had waited so long to see.

She started to run towards him. "Petroc! Petroc, it's us!"

All at once they were together. Petroc lifted her right off the ground and swung her round.

"Morwen, I never thought to see you again! And Luke, and Rosie too."

"What has happened, Petroc? How did you escape? And Salvis..."

"Salvis is dead," Petroc sighed, setting his sister down. "Bellum killed him with his own sword on the platform in the centre of the courtyard for all to see. And all who were held captive by Bellum are now set free."

Morwen sank to the ground and covered her face with her hands and Rosie burst into tears. Only

Luke stood, white faced, saying nothing. There seemed nothing to say.

As they waited, the sun came up. Night was over. A new day had dawned.

Chapter 17

Bright morning star

Petroc and Luke were skimming pebbles into the sea to find out who could throw the furthest. Once Petroc would have won easily, but the last few months had left him thin and weak and now the two boys were evenly matched.

He had shared very little about what had happened to him and Luke was wise enough not to ask, but he hated to see his friend looking so ill. Many times he thought that if Salvis were here he would heal Petroc. Only Salvis wasn't here any more and there was nothing anyone could do.

After his death there had seemed nothing to do but to return to the Bay of Dolphins. The rest of the "army" had gone back to their cottages and farms. Only the four of them, Petroc and Luke, Morwen and Rosie, stayed in Kett's house with Martha and Delfi, who was so ashamed of what her father had done that she would not leave the house. Josh had disappeared. Some said he was with Bellum still, others that he had regretted what he had done and leapt off the cliffs over by Black Rock Bay. No one knew the truth and probably no one ever would.

No one knew what to do either. The four of them spent much of their time on the beach. The girls were now looking for shells in the rock pools. They were all too full of sorrow for Salvis to even think of what they should do.

Bellum was quiet, although his stronghold still stood firm. It was as though Karensa held its breath waiting for something to happen, but no one knew what they were waiting for.

The only thing Petroc had told them about Bellum and Carrik was that what they had done to him was nothing compared with what they had done to others.

Petroc had watched Salvis die, but he would not speak of it, not even to Luke. He would only say that Bellum had killed him with his own sword.

Delfi remained close to Martha's side, still ashamed at what her father had done. Luke felt sorry for her, but he could not bring himself to tell her so.

As for Luke, his thoughts were everywhere at once. He was ashamed that when the testing time had come he had run away, and for the first time in months he longed with all his heart to go home. He looked out to sea and saw Telki and Praze racing through the waves, their smooth grey bodies sending up rainbows of coloured spray that sparkled in the afternoon sunlight.

"I wish you had never brought me here!" he called to the dolphins. "Why did you? Why did you do it? Why did you bother?"

"They were obeying the King," said a quiet voice behind him.

Luke span round. A tall, slim man dressed in grey stood behind him.

"Salvis? Salvis, but it can't be! You... you're..."

Petroc had joined them. "It must be a ghost," he muttered. "It must be! I saw him die!"

The girls were there too. Lord Salvis threw back his head and laughed, picking Rosie up under one arm and Morwen under the other and he swung them around and around.

"Can a ghost do this?" he cried and now his voice held all the power of creation.

He set them down. Morwen began to laugh joyfully. "Salvis, Salvis, you didn't die!"

"Oh I did," Salvis replied, suddenly serious. "That really was me, Petroc, and Bellum's sword really did pierce my heart. Now I can die no more and all who trust in me shall not die. The battle is won, my children. Whatever Bellum does now he can never gain victory."

Luke's heart began to beat very, very fast, then slowly, then fast again for he realised Salvis' true identity.

"That means you, you are..." the explanation was so awesome that he was unable to say the words.

Salvis helped him. "My name means Saviour. And yes, you do know me by another name, my true name. I am the First and Last. I was here before Time began and I will go on after Time is ended. I am the Bright Morning Star."

Later, when they had all become used to the idea that Lord Salvis was alive, he shared secrets with them plainly so that they could understand. Then, he asked Luke to come for a walk with him along the beach, and they found a sheltered spot where they could sit on the rocks and feel the sun warm on their faces.

Luke looked down at the sand. Someone must

have told Lord Salvis that he had denied him and run away, but who knew except for himself?

"Luke, have you learnt that lesson yet?" Salvis asked.

The boy did not have to think about it, he knew what the lesson was.

"Yes, I have, Lord."

"What have you learnt?"

Luke hung his head, unable to look the Lord in the eye. "I've learnt not to judge people, Lord. That I'm no better than anyone else. And to forgive."

"Then you are ready to go home."

He nodded. "Lord, my mum, she didn't want to leave me, did she?"

"Of course not." Salvis put a gentle hand on his shoulder. "She was very, very ill, Luke. That was why she died. Leaving you and Rosie was the last thing she wanted in all the world. She prayed that you would find peace in your heart one day. You have to forgive her, Luke... just as I have to forgive you for running away."

Luke gave a sigh that became a sob, a deep heart's cry he had hidden for years.

"Lord, I'm so sorry. Not just for that. For all the things I've done wrong. For... for being horrible to Stacey and getting into trouble with the police and for taking the boat out when I shouldn't and..." the things he had done wrong came tumbling from him like a river in flood. Then, he looked up at Salvis, whose brown eyes were full of compassion, "Lord," Luke whispered. "Lord, please forgive me. And... and I don't want to go home. I want to stay here with you for ever."

"You cannot stay here any longer. You have a

118

job to do in your world. And I promise that I will always be in your heart."

"Lord?"

"When you get home, find the book that your mother cherished above all others. Read it carefully and I will give you the power to understand. In that book is the true story about me. Tell others about me. That is the work I have for you, for you and Rosie, but especially for you."

"What will you do, Lord? Will you defeat Bellum?"

"I already have. I gave my life so that the people who turned away from the King did not have to be punished. For now, things will stay as they are. Bellum will still lure people into his stronghold but I will be seated in the Royal Palace so that those who want to may enter, just as they did in the days before they disobeyed. But one day I shall ride out of the Royal Palace again and then Bellum will be banished forever."

"How long will that be, Lord?" Luke wondered if he might possibly stay on Karensa until it was done.

"Only my Father, the King, knows that," Lord Salvis smiled. "Now, look over by the cliffs."

By the little path that led up the cliff to Kett's house, rocking gently in shallow water, was their own dinghy. The oars were in place ready to go.

"But what of the mist, Lord? Shouldn't we wait for it to clear?"

"Not this time. Telki and Praze will guide you back to Cornwall. Find Rosie and say goodbye to your friends."

Leaving Petroc was hardest of all. They had only

just met again after so long.

"D'you remember that day we went to Black Rock Bay?" Petroc said, grinning shakily as they clasped hands.

Luke nodded miserably, too sad to speak.

"Well," said Petroc, understanding how he felt. "Maybe it is better so."

Morwen held him tightly. "I shall miss you so," she whispered. "I wish you did not have to go. I wish you could stay here for always. I shall be so lonely when you're gone."

But Rosie was already pulling him towards the boat, scared he would change his mind.

"Luke, we'll see Dad again! Think how worried they've been. They must have been looking everywhere for us."

She need not have been concerned. Luke knew where he belonged. Soon the little boat was moving through the water towards the mist.

They looked back to the shore. Petroc and Morwen stood alone. Lord Salvis had gone.

"Telki, Praze!" Luke called. "Thank you for bringing us here safely! Now take us home!"

The dolphins leapt joyfully through the waves as they led them into the mist. Luke and Rosie laughed aloud as the dolphin's joy matched the joy they felt in their own hearts as they set out for home.

Chapter 18

Towards the dawn

The beach seemed just the same.

Luke and Rosie looked at each other in astonishment.

"Luke," Rosie cried. "Your clothes, your hair!"

Luke looked at his feet. He was wearing his old trainers. And his T-shirt. And his shorts. He put a hand up to his neck. It was bare. His hair was cut short.

Rosie was in her old clothes too, her fair hair loose and curly and blowing in her eyes just as it had the day they left Poldawn.

"What's happened to us, Luke? Was it a dream?"

"I don't know, but you'd think we'd never been away."

He was right. The day was hot and sunny, just as it had been when they left. The mist they had just travelled through was gone and they could clearly see the horizon. There was no sign of Karensa.

He rowed up the inlet and pulled the boat back to its mooring, steadying it for Rosie to jump out, and then he secured it. The rope was there as they had left it, just as Luke had impatiently thrown it in his hurry to get away.

Luke followed her. The cottage seemed the same too. Dad was in the garden, painting the fence.

Rosie sprang down the garden path and leapt to

him, her arms wide. "Dad, Dad, it's us! It's me! We're home."

Dad laughed. "Anyone would think you'd been away for months. Did you have a good boat trip? I hope you didn't go out too far."

"But we have, Dad," Rosie said. "We've been away almost a year."

Dad chuckled. "Go on with you, even Luke doesn't row that slowly! Go and find Stacey... She's in the kitchen baking. Go and see what she's made. It's your favourite. No Luke, not you. I want to talk to you."

Rosie skipped up the path as if nothing had happened to them, but before she went inside she turned and smiled at her brother and everything they had been through together, the good times and the bad, was in her smile.

Luke looked up at his father but before his dad could speak he said, "I'm sorry. I was wrong, Dad. About Stacey, I was wrong. I'm going to say sorry to her, too."

"You don't need to, Luke," said a soft voice behind him and there was Stacey with a plate of freshly-baked cakes in her hand.

"I'm going to say it anyway. I am sorry, Stacey. I know I've been a real pain. Can we start again from now?"

"We just did," Stacey replied.

Then she started to cry and Dad looked as if he wanted to cry, but didn't and Rosie, as always, cried too and they all hugged each other and the cakes ended up on the grass.

"It won't matter," Luke said. "We'll dust them off and eat them!"

Much later, when Luke and Rosie were on their own and all the excitement had died down, they tried to make sense out of what had happened.

"It's like we've never been away," Luke said. "It's like... like there never was a Karensa... or Petroc or Morwen or... or... Salvis.."

Once again Rosie brushed away a tear. She seemed to be doing a lot of that these days.

"I shall miss them, especially Salvis... Did it really happen, Luke? Maybe it was just a dream?"

Wonderingly, Luke lifted up his T-shirt. On his shoulder was the white scar where he had fallen on a branch that day he and Kett had tried to rescue Petroc.

"No, Rosie," he said. "It was real."

"I know," she said suddenly. "We'll get the map out and see if we can find Karensa on it. Most of the islands are marked."

They raced upstairs to the study and took down the heavy road atlas. Luke found the page.

"No, not one of these is called Karensa."

"Wait a minute, what's this?" Rosie had pulled out another book. She read the title. "A history of ancient names. How do you spell Karensa? Is it a K or a C ?"

"Give it here... Look, here it is... Karensa... a name that means peace."

"Peace! Karensa, Island of Peace!"

"It wasn't Karensa that was the peace," Luke replied. "It was Salvis. Oh Rosie, how shall we live without Salvis?"

And he was there. They didn't see him but they knew he was there with them. His peace was everywhere.

"Oh," Rosie breathed. "Oh Salvis, is it really you?"

A voice in Luke's heart reminded him of what Salvis had said just before they had left for home. Frantically he began to search the book shelves until he found what he was looking for: the Bible his mother had kept beside her bed and read each night before she went to sleep. This must be the cherished book that Salvis had referred to.

Brother and sister sat on Luke's bed and looked at it together. A bookmark had been left in the section called the Gospel of John, about three quarters of the way through, in the part called the New Testament.

"Look at this," Luke read excitedly. "John chapter one says, 'In the beginning was the Word and the Word was with God and the Word was God...'

"The King said about the word," Rosie interrupted excitedly. "He said his word could defeat Bellum..."

"Ssh, listen... This... this is Salvis in this book. I just know it... Only he isn't called Salvis and Bellum isn't called Bellum... This Jesus, he's God's son and he was innocent, yet he died for us who are guilty, to set us free, just like the people were set free from Bellum's stronghold when Salvis died. It all makes sense now!"

"And Jesus came back to life again. We learnt that at school."

"Rosie, we've got to tell people about this. We've got to tell people so they can know Salvis... I mean Jesus... When I said I was sorry to him I felt everything change."

"But I didn't do that," Rosie said slowly.

"Why not do it now? He's here. We just can't see

him, that's all."

"But I don't feel like you do!"

"You will. Just say you're sorry and ask him into your life to be your Lord and friend."

Rosie closed her eyes tight. She did as Luke had said and when she opened her eyes again she whispered, "Oh Luke, he is here. I can feel him too. I know he's beside me and a part of me."

That night Luke stood by the open bedroom window and he wasn't surprised when his sister joined him.

"I can't sleep," she said.

"Me neither. The duvet feels funny."

Rosie giggled. "It does after all those furs and that straw. I like a duvet best... and clean sheets are nice... and Stacey's cakes..."

"And the chips we had for tea."

"Look at the stars... Luke, there's one moving across the sky."

"Salvis said he was the Bright Morning Star."

And once again he was there. The whole room was filled with his peace and he seemed to say to them, "One day, my children, you will come back to me here."

Luke fetched the Bible from his bedside table. He found that suddenly he wanted to read it. What was more he could understand it. Things that would have seemed difficult before were made plain.

He'd noticed that Stacey had been to the small chapel in Poldawn two or three times, so perhaps she believed in Jesus too. He remembered going to church with his parents when he was much younger, but after his mother had died his dad hadn't wanted to go any more. Perhaps things would be different now. Maybe Stacey would take them to church? He wanted to know if there were other people who knew Jesus like he did. He wanted to tell people who didn't know him just how great he was. His dad. His friends, everyone...

They didn't sleep that first night, but sat at the window talking and watching the sky get lighter as morning came.

"What are they doing now?" Rosie sighed as the first streaks of light gave the sky a pink glow. "Delfi, Morwen, Petroc, Martha... The land for broken dreams, Luke... The place the aching heart knows.."

"Where sea birds fly from rocks of gold,
"And dolphins race with rainbows."

"Look at that star now. It's picked up speed."

Together they watched as the Bright Morning Star moved across the sky towards the dawn.

THE END...

OR THE BEGINNING?

The later books in the Tales of Karensa *series...*

Castle of Shadows
Jean Cullop

The King gave a loud cry, a cry that resounded through the entire universe. "Now my Son who was dead is alive again! Now my people can come to me once more! Now, Salvis, you wear your royal robes... One day you will judge the people of Karensa and from now onward all those who trust in you will be welcomed into the Royal Palace. Meanwhile, let the battle continue. Now my people must choose whom they will follow and Bellum will try everything in his power to keep them from coming to me. My friends, this is where the real conflict starts."

Veritan lifted high the golden sword of truth and a great and mightly call to arms resounded around the Hall and was carried to the ends of the Earth.

ISBN 1 85999 463 6

Children of the Second Morning
Jean Cullop

Rosie hesitated by the wooden door. "Luke, think! If we go through there we may not be able to get back! At least not for ages. Remember last time. We were on Karensa for nearly a year. Think of the dangers, Luke! Think of sleeping on straw mattresses! Think of boring food and no telly, and work instead of school... and there are other dangers on Karensa. Think about Bellum!"

Luke closed his eyes, trying to make sense of his thoughts. Karensa was calling him. Salvis was calling him. It was like going home. The call on his life was strong and he couldn't deny it.

He felt Salvis close to them, so close that he could almost feel his great heart beating. Just to be there, on Karensa again... The call became stronger and stronger.

ISBN 1 85999 526 8

Silver Serpent, Golden Sword
Jean Cullop

"This is the golden sword of truth, which can never be defeated in battle," said Lord Veritan. "The coming times will be very hard for the King's people. I am here to prepare you for battle. Lord Bellum and the Guardians have taken the silver serpent as their emblem, but that serpent will never overcome the golden sword. Now, you must all kneel."

He passed the mighty sword over their heads, so close that its two-edged blade touched their hair. As the sword moved, the light of day deepened to that of a glorious sunset.

When it was done, and daylight returned, Veritan spoke even more seriously. "The truth of the King's word will be your protection. Some of you will be called to suffer for your loyalty to the King..."

ISBN 1 85999 555 1